THE DROP

Also by Mark Lee Golden

A Ring of Torrents: A Jewish Mary

The Drop

SECRET DELIVERY

Mark Lee Golden

Fancy Minds
Spokane, Washington

Covers inspired by photos from Joyce Wilkens' book
Tea Cup Art. Special thanks to her.

Special thanks to Judy Windfield, Paul W. Peterson,
John Reeves and Ruth Danner for help in editing and
advice.

Also, hats off to the Visual Thesaurus.

Published by Fancy Minds, Spokane, WA

markleegoldenwriter.com
mark@markleegoldenwriter.com
Also Illustrated Words.com

Falling into a slippery rabbit hole—feet first.
Did someone trip me? Someone I didn't know?
On the way down—I grasp a mystery.
Why is this rabbit hole furnished with fluorescent lights?

Manhattan

Dawn rises over one of the largest and advanced cities in the world. Millions of inhabitants see the wondrous gleam of a modern palette reflecting on over 100,000 window panes. The inspiring edifice stands tall, proud and strong. Packed tightly, the people begin their circuit of responsibilities. Immigrants, transplanted races, cultures and tongues push on the day's purposes once more. The beauty and variety of structures receive and disperse the busy population. A valid piece of the epitome of mankind's creative architecture confronts the Atlantic. On certain days the hundreds of buildings and spires really do scrape the sky, providing a memorable skyline seen by millions of tourists. One might assume skyscrapers and highrises cast immense shadows vying with each other to allow as little direct sunlight to the people.

Manhattan Island is bounded by the Hudson, East and Harlem rivers. It is one of the five boroughs of New York City. The island is 13.4 miles long and 2.3 miles at its widest. The 23 square miles now has roughly 1,640,000 residents… 1,640,000 identities. That's 72,033 residents per square mile. On business days, the influx of commuters increases the island's number to over 3.9 million. It's the most densely populated U.S. county, and also one of the most densely populated areas in the world. Here among many of the world's languages one can find every kind of food and restaurant. Manhattan is an urbanized microcosm of the globe.

The island is now among the world's major commercial, financial and cultural centers and hosts the United Nations Headquarters. It is home to the world's two largest stock exchanges.

In far centuries past, the Lenape Native Americans people paddled canoes and rustic watercraft here. Now 31 bridges and tunnels connect to the outside world.

Dutch colonists purchased the island (which in today's money cost $1,050), in 1626 from the Canarsee Indians of the Lenape. The chief of the Canarsees happily accepted trade goods in exchange for the island, which the Weckquaesgeeks tribe actually controlled. The isle of New Netherland was in Dutch hands for 40 years. Then the English took the island, renaming it New York. Now, it, along with the surrounding metropolis, is perhaps the most widely known city around the world.

The island city is known for its public landmarks. Created in the mid-1800s, Central Park, the famous greenspace, covers 843 acres. It's an urban oasis of trees, gardens, rolling meadows, arches, sculptures, statues and vistas. Outdoor activities include hiking, biking, ice-skating, picnicking, and listening to live concerts.

The world met, meets, and will always venture here. Yet in storms and in fair weather, unseen and not recognized visitors walk the pavements. Not all are of this world.

- PART ONE -

Prologue

One Month After the Christmas Attack

Lissa Ryons never liked hospital rooms. And so, doctors and nurses quickly learned to dodge her difficult ways.

She resented the white-clothed emissaries of goodness, as they played their mysterious masters of medical puzzles with the human body—now her body. Thoughts of this exclusive club of total strangers looking at, probing in, tapping on, and sticking needles where they deemed necessary, made her queasy. Caught in such experiments and so-so diagnoses made such professionals seem too powerful. Lissa felt like a helpless five year old in a middle-aged woman's body, but without her mommy to comfort her.

When Lissa regained semi-consciousness, pain rang like lots of loud doorbells ringing at the same time. She tried to shout. But in her medicated state, only slurred words tumbled out in disoriented phrases. Lissa's thinking wobbled between morphine's half-dreams and the perplexing presence of sharp pain.

Then the beep and bell sounds, the real ones, the ones outside of her body caught her attention. "Answer-r-r dah dam…door some…one! Who-hoo. Hoo, the hahhh...ell is ring-ging that d-d-door…beh-beh-bell?"

She would have been embarrassed if she knew this tirade was being videotaped for employee training purposes.

An RN, checking the IV bag, heart rate, and other devices making beeps and bell sounds, stopped and looked intently at Lissa. The nurse's heart went out to the woman whose eyes lay closed, mind fumbling, and a dry tongue trying to gain control and communicate. The evening shift's critical-care nurse name tag read "Lucy."

The RN spoke in a soothing voice, "Miss Ryons, ahh…Doctor Ryons. How are you doing?" Then, in a practiced, up-tempo tone, "Can you open your eyes for me, hun?"

Open my eyes? Lissa sloshed and fumbled through her messy mental files wondering what that meant. Eyes fluttering, she blurted in the direction of the voice, "Turrn awff dem dam doors bells frrist!"

Lucy considered her options while electronically raising the bed and fluffing pillows. She barely heard the constant beeps, bells and what-not. Regrettably, they didn't come with volume controls. These sounds were beyond second nature to her. Seven years in ICU could make personnel have hearing like a fox in the wild, with sensitized ears catching and dismissing the unimportant routine sounds. The pertinent spikes or lulls—these pricked the trained ears.

"Doctor Ryons, you've been in an accident. You're in a hospital. The confusion and grogginess are from the medications." Lucy had given that speech countless times during her career. "Just rest now. The noisy bells are medical equipment doing their job."

Lissa didn't see the nurse's caring smile. She dozed off; one of many such brief awakenings.

* * *

Days later, Lissa overheard a man and a woman talking nearby. The voice of the man belonged to Lars Lofgren, part of Dr. Ryons' U.N. laboratory crew. Nurse Lucy said, "The dosages of her meds will be lowered today and she will start to be more her usual self over the next week. She'll steadily become more conscious as the days go by. Patients surviving this kind of trauma usually remember little if anything of the circumstances that led up to and caused their injuries. The final week or two will be spent three floors down in the medical care unit. The RNs are pretty good there.

"Also, though not uncommon, she has done her share of half-awake ICU mumbling as we call it. Several times she has spoken in her sleep about a 'stage car go.' Also, something about 'eyes' really bugs her. Don't know what that means, but it seems important to her."

Lars said, "'Stage car go?' Yah, you got me on that one, nurse. 'Eyes?' We all got 'em." Then he put these two linked mysteries out of his mind.

Although Lissa heard bits of the conversation, these meant nothing to her. She drifted back to sleep.

* * *

Dr. Lissa Ryons ran the U.N. Headquarters Forensics Department. A middle-aged, French Canadian, now living in New York City, employed at the United Nations for the last three years. Ryons, a better-than-average looking woman and divorcee, wasn't dating at present. Her slim curvy figure, longer than shoulder length wavy auburn hair, and pretty green eyes, caused the occasional compliment and second-looks from men.

A private person. Little was known about her life outside of the sterile, all-business demeanor she arrives at 9 a.m. each day.

Her three grown children live nowhere near the Northeast. She enjoys the freedom of having no pets or family responsibilities. The doctor puts in an extra hour or two at the lab when she wants, which happens more and more often. Though she terms it 'dedication,' others called it 'loneliness or boredom' due to no social life. She liked a bumper sticker which read, 'I THINK! Therefore, I AM SINGLE.'

She has mused, "I never come to the U.N. on Sunday." But, there was a little tug of regret in reflecting at that statement.

Her years of higher education and top-drawer referrals from previous employers, easily landed her this job, which she enjoyed. "I'm not a nerd," she told herself on occasion, like on empty Saturday nights, "Just a curious woman who has lost her curiosity for men."

A naturally inquisitive person, Lissa Ryons was good at noticing things—except people—especially when it came to their needs and emotions.

Her favorite color was grey.

Chapter 1

Lars Lofgren, began his employment at the United Nations Forensics Laboratory, two years before Dr. Lissa Ryons took her leadership post. A Norwegian immigrant, in his late-thirties, Lars was tall, sturdy and blond. He wore a reddish blond neatly trimmed beard, spoke good English, was kind, clever and resourceful. Lars was happy to be in the United States. At the lab, when a problem proved too complex for him, Dr. Ryons appreciated that he respected teamwork and the line of authority.

Whenever weather permitted, Lars walked or rode his bicycle to work. On the way home, he took pleasure in the exercise after being indoors all day. Several years ago he married a U.N. receptionist, from Ecuador, named Adelina, who worked only a few floors down from Forensics. Often his wife joined him for lunch if their schedules permitted; a small perk for working at the same address. They'd met in the United Nations commissary two years before and their romance blossomed. Lars used to remark, "Sweetie, if only these countries could find love here too, then we'd truly have a better, more united world." A heartfelt grin always followed.

After the attack, that playful jest emptied out of his heart.

* * *

Of the five workers in the lab, Lars and Lissa had developed a faintly pleasant working relationship. He often invited her to have lunch in the commissary with him and his wife, Adelina. But Lissa turned down each offer without giving a reason. One day at lunch, from across the room, their eyes met. Like prey caught, Dr. Ryons managed a leave-me-alone smile. But Lars and Adelina moved to where she was sitting—the awkwardness which followed made this a onetime only event. Since then though, in-house small talk turned a mere degree warmer between boss and coworker.

Lars' usual route home from work made it convenient for him to stop at the hospital. Early after the attack, he visited a few times, but only saw Lissa's battered, sleeping shape and the tubes running in and out of her body. He became the unofficial U.N. staff reporter, updating those at work on her progress.

One day, to his surprise, Dr. Ryons woke, fully opening her eyes. In a slow, scratchy voice she mumbled, "I was dream...ing. Dreaming how, when you meet people—some people—for the first time, they'll say 'Pleased to meet you.' They don't even mean it; they are just saying it to be po...po...lite." In an instant her eyes shut and she fell into a snuffling snore. Dr. Ryons wouldn't remember this quick dissertation, or Lars' visit.

After that odd critique on human nature, he turned and left.

On another visit, this time with his wife, Lissa woke and mumbled in a profound-sounding voice. "Lars…it must ahh just been ahh dream, rock n' roll in the 60s and 70s. The musicians didn't have long hair, no one did. No one! The whole long hair fad never happened.

"Instead, they were all into shoe wear, amazing shoe wear. Everybody thought the way to be different and cool was shoes. No crazy heads of hair back then. So, ah…the whole fashion footwear market had an eruption. Yeah, yeah, I know, wild shoes were a fad for a time; platform shoes and all that. Imagine, more like Alice in Wonderlace. Rock stars led the way into bizarre styles, colors, sizes, heights—everything! Even clown shoes and bowling shoes were popular. Funny, hah? Webell shoes, too! I mean rrr...rebel shoes.

"Shoes, shoes, shoes! All the young men of those decades wore the same length hair as their dads...and it was cool. Enormous and crazily colored, mutated shooozs..."

She was out again, head laying deep in the pillow. Lars looked down at Dr. Ryons for whom he held sincere respect. He regretted this role of a waiting messenger, burdened with frustrating, life-changing news. Lars stared silently at her swollen face, yellow, blue, black. His news again would have to wait.

Adelina hugged him and rested her head on his chest, not being tall enough to reach his shoulder. In her high feminine voice she said, "Honey, why do you visit her, I mean, besides being your boss?"

"Because she is close to no one."

For this, Adelina squeezed him. Eyes gleaming with admiration, she looked up at him and they left.

* * *

Lars was there the day Lissa's mind cleared, recovering full consciousness. Head on pillow, she looked at him and then around the room. In a bewildered, tired voice, she asked, "What happened? What day is it? Why am I in the hospital, Lars? These tubes and all the machines!" She paused. "And why are you here?"

He didn't answer. His eyes moved from her face to the floor for a long moment. If an instant could make something terrible go away, he wouldn't have looked up as soon as he did. The thought of delivering this news had plagued his mind, and now the time to tell it was inescapable.

With a loud "Ouch!" Dr. Ryons raised her upper body by her elbows and leaned slightly forward. "Why am I in a hospital?" With a gulp of air which scrunched up one side of her face, she voiced a faint, "Why?"

He decided to venture with a good natured opening, "I'm so glad to see you well, and coherent Dr. Ryons. I've waited for this day...for your recovery." Then he followed with relaying the greetings from the lab crew, adding, "The crew has received hospital updates from me. We signed, and sent a get-well-soon card weeks ago, hoping for your full recovery and return." Lars pointed to the open card on a counter top. He heaved a sigh and exhaled a gust filled with grief. Dr. Ryons found the bed's adjustment controls and raised herself to get a closer view of him and scrutinize his expressions.

Lars began placing together the puzzle pieces that were now history—forever part of New York City's history and America's. "There were eight Islamic terrorists in front of the U.N. They killed themselves and took others' lives for...for their religion or whatever. I saw them protesting when I went home, but they were just another bunch of who-evers...on a different day. Y' know how it is." He looked around her room focusing on nothing. "Anyway, three men disguised themselves, dressing as women...un...under their bur...burkas...they had huge suicide vests." Lars' eyes teared up, he choked and took a breath. "Together, all three murderers ran toward the main entrance. When the security guards saw trouble coming they fired their guns. The terrorists shouted 'Allah hu Akbar!' and entered Muslim heaven, taking both guards and many other innocent people with them. They blew up the front of the building...torn open."

Gripping the bed's hand rail Lars let his moist eyes pour out their liquid. He noticed a tissue box on a nearby counter and took several. While wiping his eyes, almost as an addendum he choked out, "...it's still being rebuilt."

"Wha…wha, wha-tut? The…oh, my gawd, the U.N.?" She groaned, trying to sit up farther, then fell back. "Oh, no! My God, no! Lars! Tell me it's not true. Please!" The words came out of her mouth hopeless as a litter of premature puppies, dying. Realizing she and death had passed by each other so closely, Lissa's body jerked. She tried to squeeze herself tight, vainly wanting to protect every inch, but the tubes in and on her arms stopped her.

Lars said nothing. He bent his head low, not wanting to keep eye contact.

A nurse came by on a routine check-in and with quick recognition discreetly closed the curtain around the bed, whispering, "I'll come back shortly."

Dr. Ryons' numbing unbelief slid away. While staring straight ahead, half-mumbling to herself she spoke, "God is…great?"

Her head turned to one side of the pillow, eyes closed, mind on overload. She needed more comfort, and lowered the bed. But, angry depression surrounded her every thought and reaching for her soul, easily found it.

"Lars, I remember leaving the lab." In her imagination, an image of a pair of eyes and a slit in dark cloth, consumed her. She knew now that the Islamic head-covering had been used as a mask of evil. *Nothing but ashes now.* She shook her head as if to dispose of the memory. Those menacing, calculating eyes, held a fuse, then lit it. *My home, my place of refuge, turned into an ashen corpse, a heap of rubble.*

Lars became concerned, seeing her blood pressure numbers climb. He poured water for her and by a shaky hand held out a cup, which she didn't acknowledge.

Dr. Ryons murmured, "Another dead warrior for Islam." She remembered that moment, but the rest of the evening was only blurry fragments, scattered pieces of memory. After minutes of awkward, mutual silence, she whispered the word "Magic…" from her parched throat.

Curious, and seeing no connection, Lars asked, "Why did you say that?"

Drearily, she replied, "Huh? Oh, I-I, don't…I don't know." The word's meaning slid to a vague, unreachable place in her memory, then dissipated.

Dr. Ryons recalled passing the two swing-shift security guards month after month, never knowing their names or caring anything about either one of them. Now, a realization settled on her concerning the men and their jobs…so different from hers. *They would have protected my worthless ass with their lives if it came to that. Damn! I can be so impersonal.* She lay in silent panic trying to imagine the destruction to the physical edifice of mankind's symbolic potential; *the United Nations: a fabled, peaceful world of united countries.*

Lars' set the cup on the side tray. His hands fidgeted while he decided if this visit would do for today or to go on. He needed to get it over with and continued, "You were almost a safe distance away when the explosives went off."

Dilemma strained her heart. "Then how, how…how did I survive?" *I almost died?*

"The taxi you started to enter, protected you. Unfortunately, the driver was killed by glass shards from the car's windows. You must've ducked at just the right second. The first responders found you unconscious on the street, bleeding with a bad concussion, and probable internal injuries. Oh, you did have fractures. Doctor, you were the only one near the blast who survived. Those in the upper floors heard a thud noise followed by rumbling and then the building shudder."

He paused, searching for what was relevant. "It's been like 9/11. Forty seven people died, victims of different nationalities. Some were in the lobby, others on the first few floors above. Lucky ones were simply knocked off their feet. The entire U.N. Complex was in lockdown for days. Only skeleton crews kept the facilities running, each had an armed escort. The biggest news for weeks. The United Nations Christmas bombing is what the media has labeled 'The Tragedy.'"

Forcefully, Dr. Ryons pressed the button to raise her bed up all the way and stretched forward. In great pain, she shrieked, "For weeks! Weeks? How long have I…." She slumped back on the bed and trailed off, silently attempting to do the gruesome math.

A nurse opened the curtain, and eyed Lars. "Sir, give it one more minute, then she should rest. A doctor will be along shortly." The nurse left the curtain part way open.

He nodded. Lars informed Dr. Ryons as sensitively as possible. "Because you suffered serious swelling of the brain, the medical team, after much deliberation—I must add—concluded you needed to be placed into a medically induced coma-state. The doctors here have treated you…well…it's almost a miracle…you are going to fully recover with some months of out-patient care. Head injuries are tough going."

Dr. Ryons nodded in neutral resignation. She was impressed that someone from work would visit her out of good old compassion. But it was unlike her to go to that place inside where *Thanks!* came from. Instead, feeling five years old again and Mommy nowhere in sight, with a slight sneer, and nostrils flared, she said, "Sounds like you know everything about me!" She closed her eyes as desperation closed her heart.

Chapter 2

Late February

The day before Dr. Ryons' release, two representatives from the United Nations Employee Commons Department visited her. Ryons thought it peculiar that the U.N. hadn't sent any officials before. Agents from the FBI had interviewed her twice.

Now, a middle-aged, well-groomed, suited man, who spoke with a faint Scottish accent, entered her room. Followed by a brown skinned woman who wore a bright colored African dress and a fabric head wrap; she spoke with a foreign accent. They introduced themselves. After expressing sympathetic comments, the woman closed the door to Dr. Ryons private room. The man, Jonathan Javan, pulled a chair close to Lissa. The woman, Miss Cahni Olletey, stood at the foot of the bed.

Mr. Javan spoke in a serious, decisive tone. "Dr. Ryons, due to your unfortunate injuries, time in the coma or sedated, your time to watch the news has been little. You've probably missed a fine point in understanding the explosion at the U.N. That is why we are here today. When you leave the hospital premises and spend the week at home recuperating we'd like … rather we insist on providing you a bodyguard. You might further desire this protection after your return to work as well."

Ryons, all ears, perked up at this. She winced as her tiny hairs stood on end and her skin went in a prickly goosepimply way. "Whaat?"

He continued. "We do not believe you to be in any physical harm. Nothing of a revenge or retaliation attack for your having survived, no. But, you will certainly be sought after by the media.

Press, bloggers, and ambulance chaser writers want you. These people are persistent, and have one goal—to get you to talk. Of course you are free to comply with them. Dr. Ryons, your bodyguard's job is not political. His sworn duty is your quality of life—think of the paparazzi chasing you. Not fun. He's yours to direct. But please take advantage of his discretion for privacy. Also, he's worn the peacekeepers' blue helmet, but served in the U.S. military before that. Tomorrow, there will be police when you exit the hospital. They will have secured a taxi with a plain clothes officer doing the driving to your apartment building. Your bodyguard takes up his position at the street level entry door which we know is always locked. No one gets in without his inspection. If you want to go anywhere, he goes with you. He can have errands performed for you. Or, items can be delivered, take-out and such."

Lissa grinned, "Sounds like a stakeout. Oh goody."

Miss Olletey spoke next. "At this time you are something of a local treasure, maybe even a national treasure." She looked to Javan, he nodded in agreement. "Doctor Ryons, headquarters' attack was accomplished by less than ten individuals. Law enforcement teams are investigating whether others played supporting roles of any sort. What's important is that what you say—if anything—will be heard by a waiting world. What you say could cause attacks or counter-attacks elsewhere. Do you understand?"

Ryons nodded.

Olletey continued. "Certain larger elements are at play here and the United Nations Secretary General is asking for your assistance. He sent us here after deliberation with several key members.

"Extremists followers of Islam coordinated the deadly attack at Christmas time. They do not follow the Christian tradition to celebrate the birth of Jesus—whom I add—was a Jewish baby. Did the terrorists want to dent the Christian faith worldwide? Or, was the attack, as some in the media call it, The Christmas Bombing, more about the United Nations? Was it more of an attack at international unity, the pursuit of world peace and modernization, in short, the U.N. Hmm?"

The patient used the controls to move the hospital bed and sit up all the way. "One of them had a sign with a lousy caricature of Santa Claus titled 'Satan Claus.'"

Cahni spoke in a slithery, confident way, "Interesting. That sign, if indeed true, was burnt to ashes in the conflagration which followed. The medical team here explained that your memory has taken quite a jarring—as anyone's would have." Cahni spoke an upbeat cheery tone, "It's a miracle you're alive!" She spread her arms out. "Yet, a brain mis-fires, imagines and forgets too."

Dr. Ryons deeply considered this. Innocently, she added, "Well, the surveillance cameras must've got it."

The visitors looked at each. The man spoke again. "If such a sign, put together by a small band of terrorists, was publicized, Doctor, would that be a good or a bad thing, for the public? Consider the various countries where Christians and Jews live with difficulty due to Islam's strong influence?"

A queer expression showed through Lissa's black, blue and yellowed face. She looked at both of these officials. *They are trying to control me. Is that it?*

Folding her arms as little as she could, Ryons asserted, "You doctored the film, blurred it away or something. Didn't you? Did you come here to ask me to sign a disclosure agreement, is that it?"

Cahni answered, "Our purpose her—."

The bandaged victim blurted out, "Is to make me buy in to some political correctness…isn't it?" Lissa's voice rose, "Isn't it? What have you got next, some cleric to come in from the waiting room, and explain how theirs is a religion of peace? Hope he doesn't trip over my I.V. tubes!" She huffed. "So, that's where 'The

Tragedy' label came in, no 'Christmas Bombing' here folks! Let PC reign long and prosper, oh yeah. You two, PC seems like a bad habit to me." She gave them an odd look and asked with a bitter tang, "How about Xmas Bombing, will that do?"

Stone-faced, the visitors stood by the foot of the bed, ready to leave.

At the door Jonathan pointed out, "After 30 years of bloodshed and strife in the U.K., the Irish and Northern Irish settled into referring to the decades of fighting as 'The Troubles.' The Secretary General is trying to mend the matter that befell our doorstep. All of the truth is sometimes unnecessary." He turned back as he stepped through the door. Good day, doctor."

In their final words, Lissa saw how their jobs differed from her's and the lab's. She preferred hers. Alone, Lissa huffed and rocked her head. "Mine to direct! Yeah. Gee, I get a soldier!"

Chapter 3

After a total of nine weeks, Dr. Ryons readied herself to walk out of the hospital, armed with pain meds and a stern prescription from an MD to go home from work early for the next three weeks. Due to the injury to her arm, months of twice weekly occupational therapy lay ahead of her. He provided a printout of these instructions, which to her alarm included spending one week at home, 'resting.' *What he really means is one week of house arrest!*

This MD could spot a classic over-achiever after only one brief office visit; after all he was one himself.

During her hospital stay, not one of her three children traveled to New York to visit their mother—they knew her all too well. But having arrived unconscious and then the coma, her children remained home in the states of which they resided. The RNs received the few family check-up phone calls or took a message. Her daughter sent a get-well card. One son sent flowers and a family photo. The other son only wanted her to know that he phoned. Dr. Ryons was curious about their concern and pondered their interest while reading and re-reading the scant cards and messages.

Now that she'd be released, Ryons would email them, insisting they stay home, stating, "I'm fine."

Over the years, the rare fact-finding phone calls from her children about her life or them telling her their news…well, she had always found those conventional conversations tedious. Now, she didn't want calls to become awkward interviews about her unfortunate injuries and the continuing recovery. Plus, it was an unwanted, politically mixed, media intense, episode of life. *Mixed-*

up episode is more like it! Worst of all, there is nothing on the damn TV at this hospital or probably at home. She couldn't wait to get her life back in order, get back to work. For that, she cried.

* * *

When they wheeled her down to the main floor entry she stiffened. Through the glass doors not only did she see the NYPD dark blue uniforms, she saw three TV station vans. Individuals with film and recording devices stood crammed in the waiting group of strangers. Her upper body drew back and she looked for a detour. A nurse helped her up and led her to the sliding doors. Then a policeman took possession of her bag of belongings. Another reached out to help steady Lissa.

A U.N. spokesperson waved his arms to gain attention and addressed the small crowd. Reading from a printout, he sounded firm and forbidding. "Everyone listen up! The Secretary General requests that you treat our recuperating employee as someone of no interest. She will not be providing any interviews or communication with the media until an unknown date in the future. He requests that you respect her privacy and the still fragile state of her body. As to her being moved to her residence, one our best soldiers, who is armed, will defy any attempts at contacting her. The U.N. website has the same request along with additional information about The Tragedy. Thank you for your understanding."

A police officer said, "Professor, let me get you to your taxi. Don't worry about these media folks. Try to ignore them. As planned, Bubba is waiting at the entry to your apartment building. When he talks, people do what he says. You're covered."

Professor, huh? Bubba. Who's Bubba?

Questions from loud voices and a variety of handheld microphones followed her to the taxi door. Next, a policeman placed her belongings inside. Lissa started to enter, but on a whim she turned to look at the commotion. She went into a quiet private, inner place where none of the intrusions clicked. She didn't feel the center of attraction for those few seconds in the cocoon. Emotionless, she scanned faces and equipment. She shook her head at the contrast between life in the environmentally controlled hospital room versus this chaos which stunned her. For these still moments the critical mass of publicity peaked. Shouting increased. The strangers made extra efforts for contact and response. Reporters and cameras surged toward the stationary person. Nothing they shouted touched or hooked Lissa. She turned and entered the taxi. On the news shows and websites photos of her showed a battered grim face.

Professor?

When the taxi started off, the plain clothed driver turned around and introduced himself. Then he made a cell phone call. "Hey Bubba, Lieutenant Gilroy here. On my way to deliver the package. What?" He paused. "You say no one is there. Well, let's hope it stays that way. Some might tail me. Over and out." The rest of the ride neither spoke.

When the taxi arrived at the curb of Lissa's apartment building she noticed that orange caution cones had prevented other drivers from taking the parking spot. The building had a fabric awning covering the entrance from curb to security door. Then she saw Bubba. Six-foot-five of an immense man in desert fatigues, boots, camo hat and sidearm at his waist. Seeing his brownish skin and black moustache, Lissa couldn't quite identify his origins.

Before the policeman opened his door he motioned to the bodyguard and made a signal. Pointing forefinger and index finger extended at his own eyes, he then turned his hand with the two fingers pointed at Bubba. Lissa saw the soldier look down the sidewalk both ways and then nod.

Again he turned to see Dr. Ryons. The Lieutenant said in a confident voice, "Okay Professor, we're in luck, all clear. I'll get your bags. Bubba will get your door and then carry your belongings upstairs. Once in, he will brief you on his parameters. To him you are a V.I.P., enjoy it."

In a deep voice only a big man has, he said, "Good day, Professor Ryons. Call me Bubba. We should discuss my role once I help you get settled in your living quarters." He pressed the elevator button. At her apartment door, Bubba could barely get through and needed to turn sideways and duck his head.

The bodyguard peered through all the windows and tested the curtains. He checked the strength of her front door locks. At one of the front windows facing the street and opposite buildings, Bubba waved his hand, followed by a thumbs-up.

Lissa was overwhelmed and disorientated in her home. Her head hurt. She had little ability to focus and listen. She reached her hand out to receive the printout of his parameters from the soldier. Her fingers held it, but then it drifted to the floor as she stared at nothing.

Bubba picked it up and set it on a nearby table. He'd been in combat, he knew this look. "Professor Ryons, here is a cell phone for you to use to reach me on the sidewalk. I'll take up position under the awning. Now, in the hours of midnight to 6am I'll be sacking out with my buddies across the street. They'll keep an eye open when mine are closed. Simply press any key on the phone and I or one of them will answer immediately. Ma'am, ah … do you follow?" A nod. "Okay, I'll leave you to rest. Call me for a run to get groceries and such. The U.N. covers all expenses. We're here for you. Finally, read that printout to understand my parameters for your safety." He paused. "Ma'am, do you need my assistance to get you to your bedroom. Otherwise, I'll depart." She did.

Lissa woke up mid-afternoon—hungry. Her refrigerator smelled terrible. She found Bubba's instructions and phoned him. She thought through her request and matter-of-fact said, "Bubba, this is—."

"Yes, I know who this is, Professor. What is your question?" She thought he spoke with a Caribbean accent.

"Well, I'm not a professor. I'm a scientist. Please, my U.N. title is doctor. So, could you—."

"Check, ma'am. Go on."

Lissa calmly said, "I want a new refrigerator."

"Check. Mold taken over, too unhealthy to clean. No problem. Actually, Pro—I mean Doctor Ryons, we had anticipated this need. Seven weeks unattended, whoo-hee. We'll remove and deliver your new one at eleven hundred hours tomorrow. Until then phone for take-out or have us acquire your dietary needs. Is that understood? No one but myself will come to your door with food or any toiletries, etc."

Her head spun due to medication, stress and readjusting to her own mattress. She simply said, "Yes. Check, soldier." Then an idea crossed her mind. In as much of a logical tone she could speak, she asked, "Bubba, don't you need the measurements in order to purchase the right size refrigerator?"

He answered in a formal tone. "Yes, ma'am, but we have all of that on the computer. Not a problem."

"Computer! Huh? What are you talking about?"

"Ma'am, during your comatose state in the hospital the FBI obtained a search warrant to enter your residence. They took videos and stills, dusted for fingerprints—all normal procedure—a standard sweep. The intel was loaded into their computer at HQ. They can use a laser tool to measure—"

Lissa stopped him. "What the hell for? Why were they here? How disturbing and damn annoying."

"Do you want my answer, Doctor?"

Angry, Lissa hissed and said, "Yeah, uh huh!"

"Yes, Doctor. My understanding, which is limited, this action served a two-fold purpose. One, to clear you of any direct involvement with the terrorists or terrorism. I'm sure that any electronic communication devices were cloned, such as a computer, or tablet and analyzed. They subpoenaed your cell phone records. Second, to clear your premises of any possible booby-traps planted by the terrorists to make a kill on the one who got away—you— the one America had set many hopes and prayers on. You'd be a prime target. Even the president, at a news conference, asked the nation to pray for you."

"Me? I'm not a hero, just lucky." She winced and thought, *Who the hell was praying for me, people who don't even know me. Weird.* One cheek began to twitch. "So, Bubba, answer me. Did the FBI leave any bugs behind? Are they listening to us now?"

"Ma'am, if you read through my parameters you'd find that I wouldn't be at liberty to confirm such surveillance—if true. Doctor, I hope this was a satisfactory answer."

Chapter 4

During her week-long captivity at home, she did get some much needed housecleaning done. She raced through every get well card and then disposed them all. Dr. Ryons re-acquainted herself with how a person could endlessly waste their life on the Internet. From one website to another she dug into interesting science news and tried to understand what the Facebook thing was all about. Everybody seemed to know her and yet they also wanted to be her friend anyway. She seemed to be more popular with each click. After surfing the Web for hours, she decided that taking little dips was more her style.

She settled into a routine-less, daily routine, partially fueled by the de-motivating pain medications. Occasionally, the euphoric effect of such medication made life well worth living. At least until they wore off. A forgotten bottle of Riesling helped pass the time too.

The serious injuries and fractures had healed, but ugly scabs clung to her shoulders, forehead, elbows and certain places no one would see. The unknown date of final restoration, minus scars, frustrated her. The left side of her face showed the last darkened hues of bruising; she didn't even try to cover those with make-up. Her right wrist which took the weight of her unconscious body lay snug in a brace, and her arm in a sling. Luckily, left-handed, kept her able to do certain functions.

* * *

Ryons decided to remain indoors. Her military butler and bodyguard, Bubba, phoned twice a day from under the awning. Even though he and Lissa never sat chatting over a cup of coffee, either in her apartment or at the small ground-floor lobby, she attained a level of casual consideration. On one call he told her he knew head injuries were a "bastard." He explained, "I've had 'em and I've seen 'em out in the field, ma'am."

Bubba reported if any "hostiles" attempted to buzz her apartment and gain entry. He told her, "I tell 'em, Dr. Ryons has to recuperate to regain her health. She knows how much the press wants her story and has chosen to not grant interviews to anyone until a later date. Now bug off! Then I give them my look, ma'am. No one gets passed Bubba, when I give 'em the look."

Lissa imagined a variety of faces that would make reporters and little children scatter.

He told her, "That neighbor of yours in 2C, Rosie, now she's a kind woman and the kind of woman to have as a neighbor. Pure gold. A classic sweetie."

Ryons was lost. *My white-haired problem in 2C?*

Bubba continued, "Everyday she brings me down a different homemade sweet treat and tasty hot coffee—somehow better than the way I normally make my brew. Mighty fine woman, reminds me of my granny."

Lissa took a renewed interest in the bombing, destruction and deaths. On the TV nightly news or searching Internet news sites, she viewed stories and personal accounts of the The Tragedy. Widows and widowers told tales of grief for their lost spouses, which mixed into overlapping adjectives. Each spouse was the kindest, most sincere, most generous and loving person you'd ever hope to meet. Lissa tired of the interviews. The witnesses to the explosion pretty much gave duplicating observations, too. "It was like something outta a movie or on the TV—but real! So loud! Lit up the sky! Shook all the nearby buildings! Scared me to death, I thought I was going to die. Like being in a war zone."

The U.N. released the surveillance footage of the protesters and one named U.N. employee who barely escaped death. She watched herself reach the taxi and get thrown to the pavement as a radiant flash of light and debris shot outward. The camera, a casualty, turned to static.

Shaking her head (which still ached) she watched her innocent self walk out of the U.N. having no idea of the deadly tragedy only moments away. Dr. Lissa Ryons was the lone survivor seen by millions of viewers around the world. Every time she re-watched the scenario, her body tensed. As she sat, her knees involuntarily rose to her chest and she clutched them tight. *If only I could yell at the videotape and warn myself. If only….*

Chapter 5

Beverley Roseblum lived two doors down from Dr. Ryons' apartment, in 2C. Lissa groaned at the sight of this old woman; short, curly snow-white hair, bright artificial flower on her blouse and a wrinkled face marking decades of history. Mrs. Roseblum, wood cane in hand, always greeted her neighbors with a caring and enthusiastic hello, a friendly question or compliment—sometimes all three if given the time. Lissa pegged her as a sweet old lady and wanted as little to do with her as possible. Ryons bore a slice of resentment towards someone so cheerful. She juggled common courtesy and the desire to be ignored.

Why does she have to know a thing about me? Why obligate me to answer to her disarmingly charming ways? Shouldn't she be watching TV reruns, humming old show-tunes and placing hot tea in china on yellowed lace dollies? I'm sure she's got a collection of tea cozies that would knock me over!

When Lissa moved into 2A three years ago, Mrs. Roseblum didn't just crack open her door and peer at the movers and spy on the new tenant. No, she strode down the hall, locked eyes with Lissa, stuck out her hand and said, "Put it there, neighbor!" Wincing, Lissa complied. What annoyed her was that this little old lady had a firm handshake and a warm smile, which made Lissa value herself more—an awkward feeling, one akin to having hiccupped in a full elevator. The old woman mixed outright acceptance with a "we are going to be friends" attitude. But the attitude dug deeper, more like "we get to be friends!" More hiccups would await Lissa in the following months.

After this greeting, Mrs. Roseblum tapped her cane on the floor and got out of Lissa's busy way. With a slight waddle to her gait, the old lady left and reentered 2C. Lissa wouldn't have been surprised if the elderly woman had leaped and clicked her orthopedic shoes in mid-air.

During the three years Lissa lived in her Manhattan home, dodging Mrs. Roseblum was nearly a sport. Lissa left for the U.N. the same time five days a week. Coming home varied. Weekends, Lissa stayed indoors unless she went to her lab to be alone and kill time. But the haunting neighbor remained in her mind. "I'm Mrs. Roseblum, but, you can call me Rosie. I've been roosting alone in 2C for more than thirty years. Widow. I heard you moved here from Canada. Well, knock on the door if you need anything. I'll let you be now, Lissa. Nice to have you on board."

Geez, why do people have to be so, so… invasive. You live there. I live here. Sometimes we breathe the same air. Whoopee! Life goes on.

Lissa's evasive tactics fail. She avoided using the elevator, the sound of the bell alerted Rosie to the comings and goings of neighbors. Rosie caught the secretive woman a few times in those three years. The rap of Rosie's cane handle on her door released a flurry of ill thoughts and a cringe. Many times Lissa tip-toed into the rear of her apartment and waited for the cane's thumping to die away. Lissa had conjured up an answer for every purse-in-hand and key-in-lock occurrence. When caught, she filled the moment with light hallway chatter. She turned down plenty of invitations to come for a visit, which included tea and homemade baked goods. Lissa's resistant heels dug scars into the hall carpeting.

People that are way too nice bug me. What's their problem? Let's love the world everyone! Oh yeah, so simple.

Because of the U.N. Christmas Bombing, everyone in Manhattan knew the name Doctor Lissa Ryons. With her hospital release, the update of the survivor surfaced once more on TV and

Internet. The always hospitable Mrs. Roseblum awaited the return of her victimized and timid neighbor. She had surmised over the last three years that the occupation of a forensic scientist at the U.N. might come with the inherent need for a private life. Lack of friends might be a job requirement due to political and security concerns. Nevertheless, upon Lissa's return, Mrs. Roseblum hoped to gain ground and see if there was a rusted wheel within Lissa Ryons which could grind forward. After the trauma, weeks in the hospital and arrival home, the reclusive woman in 2A might want a friend.

When Rosie cracked open her door, she noticed a huge military man holding bags while a bandaged and unsteady Lissa, one arm in a fancy sling, worked a key into her lock.

The following morning Lissa found a note from Rosie, half in and half out of the bottom of the door. The pink envelope with burgundy ribbon made it a curiosity among the pile of mail slipped through her slot. She relaxed a bit and with grudging acceptance gave in to finally visiting Mrs. Roseblum. Four days later, her feet dragged every step to 2C. *Must be the sedation of those pain meds which let my guard down. But how bad can it be?*

A wreath of dried rosebuds hung on the dark-stained wood door where a shiny brass 2C was screwed on. After a deep breath, Lissa knocked. *Did she say 30 years? Jeez, that's confinement. I expect heavy velvet Victorian curtains—closed and dim, plus that old-person urine smell, and thick burgundy carpet with trails worn by those little feet of hers.*

The door swung wide open to reveal Rosie displaying glee. "Come in, darling. Come in. What a delight!" Lissa cautiously stepped in. The door closed. "I won't bother you with a tour of my apartment, not this visit. Find a seat, anywhere you like." She stepped out of the room to click off an unseen whistling tea kettle. Then she returned and sat across from her guest. The hostess saw Lissa as an anticipated delivery of a colorful bouquet. Rosie immediately wanted to check the water level and place the vase in the sunlight, just right.

Lissa squirmed inside. *Damn, I should've taken one of those life-ain't-so-bad pain pills for this meet and greet.* She first noticed a shiny brass canister by the door with a dozen unusual polished canes in it, all fashionable and almost enviable. The apartment was like a glimpse and fragrance of spring. Bright colors adorned the walls and window coverings. No trail in the rather new looking cream colored carpeting. A computer setup with admirable accessories surprised Lissa the most. She noticed a sizable flat-screen television in the bedroom. Perhaps Lissa had misjudged the woman.

The guest eyed several dessert plates all within an arm's reach. Appetizing aromas captivated her. After a nod from her hostess Lissa vacillated in deciding what to try and how arrange them on a plate which needed to rest on her lap. Her face brightened, enjoying herself for the first time since she touched that odd lab specimen two months ago, she smiled. "Thank you. These all look so delicious. I've forgotten how much I love the smell of baking."

Rosie grinned. "Let's talk, shall we? I will tell you something about me. I met my husband at the drinking fountain at the park when I was five years old. I remember how he, like the other boys, put his cheek against the metal spout and sucked the water before it could spurt a little curving stream. We girls, being proper and dainty, drank from the stream. The boys' crude action disgusted us. Didn't they know anything about catching germs? Took me six years to break Bernie of that undignified habit." She wagged her head and chuckled.

"We grew up in a small town in Ohio. His family lived a short walk away. Our fathers worked in the same factory. Bernie was all boy, but I was all girl." She grinned, tilted her head and silence took over. Her inward eyes looked into a summer's warm swimming pond of memories. Childhood friends became school sweethearts. I remember the day I realized Bernie was a boy becoming a man. My feminine desire recognized his growing attractiveness. And he had his day when he looked me over and understood I would become a woman. The two of us liked what we saw. Something lit inside of me. It's still there today. We married one week after high school graduation. And after a short honeymoon-on-the-cheap, he told me he'd enlisted in the navy. He shipped out the next day. I was devastated. But, we needed money. This was his solution."

Lissa's heart and imagination entered into the private life made public to her. She put mental puzzle pieces together as she listened and developed a portrait of Bernie and Rosie's early years. She rarely found herself in an emotional place where people opened up to her. The china tea cup and delicate saucer slightly rattled in her one usable hand. She set it down. Rosie's sliced homemade breads and cookies lay as mere props to this pause in conversation. The two women settled into a quiet, time-free pace.

Mrs. Roseblum returned to conversing. "My husband died in a bombing." She turned to look carefully at her guest. "You survived your bombing…not my Bernie. He was only 18 years old and never knew that he left me pregnant—with triplets." Her eyes opened wide, she spoke in a knowing fashion, "Pearl Harbor." She dabbed at tears. "I never married again."

This woman is in her 90s!

On reflex, out came "Oh, I am so sorry to hear that!"

Rosie lightly chuckled. "Sorry? You had nothing to do with Pearl Harbor, I imagine. Maybe saying 'how unfortunate,' is a better sympathetic remark. I stopped the too common 'I'm sorry' thing decades ago. Makes little sense, yes, I understand the intent. But no, his young death was truly unfortunate."

Lissa gulped. She looked around at what filled the museum-like sitting room. Framed 8x10" black and white photos; a framed, tri-folded, American flag; dozens of wedding photos—each a different happy couple. Next Lissa noticed a multitude of colored photos of children, accompanied by childish gifts of finger painting, indecipherable trinkets, colorful collages, hand-cut cards and drawings "For Grandma." These filled the walls like medals and awards—all for her hostess. *My refrigerator is phase two, a huge huddled crowd of family photos and their pets, of course. Travel magnets hold most in place—all fifty states and then some.*

Lissa pondered, *All loving fans of Rosie.*

Rosie's broad smile continued below her watery eyes, which followed Lissa's roving gaze. The hostess answered unasked questions. "Ready, dear? Three children, 11 grandchildren and 22 great-grandchildren…and one is usually on the way." With a pride she added, "Mrs. Beverley Roseblum has lived a long and full life."

Composed, Lissa remarked, "You never married again? That's a lot of years, Mrs. Roseblum."

"Rosie, please. No my dear, that's a lot of love. One man for me." She wiped at a tear.

Lissa mused, *One man was too much for me.*

"One day in heaven, Bernard Roseblum will be met by our beautiful children and everyone who came after them. What a time that will be."

She reached and patted Lissa's hand. The moment passed like a warm, moist, tropical breeze gently letting itself be known. Lissa thought, *If you do see everyone in heaven, I'll be heading the other way when I see that jerk.* Following this, a refreshing spark zapped Lissa's spine. She twitched and straightened where she sat, wondering what happened. *Strong static electricity? No!*

"That vision of a grand family reunion keeps me going, dear. Ah, I also get a phone call, email, or text message from someone in the family. That helps so much, too. Our Facebook family pages go on and on. Of course they visit here paying homage to the matriarch." She chuckled.

Lissa thought heaven and such hopes were a lot of hooey. But, she had no business squelching this old lady's dreams. *What do I know of such things anyway? On the wall she's got one of those brass Christian crosses… wait. It has a Jewish star on it too. Whaat? That's messed up. I don't know what she believes.*

Rosie's vein-rumpled hand lifted off Lissa.

"Thank you for inviting me Misses—ah, Bever—I mean Rosie. I loved the lemon bars the best. I should go now. Thank you." This chat pulled something nasty out of Lissa heart. She almost volunteered, *Just by visiting, you have helped me to move past something… something old and personal."* But didn't. This remained locked behind the firewall of her heart. *After all of these years, I need to forgive that man!*

Mrs. Roseblum put together a sugary care package. Lemon bars first, then a slice of banana bread and peanut butter cookies last. Handing over the baked goods she chuckled, "From 2C to 2A, darling. Tap, tap, on my door if you ever need anything."

Well after all, it pays to visit Mrs. Roseblum. Yum!

Before closing the door Lissa asked her banged-up neighbor, "Your kids are coming to see you, right?" Lissa hung her head and a faint quiver spoke volumes to Rosie. Staring at the floor Lissa shuffled out. If she would've turned she'd have see the pained look in the ancient woman's eyes.

In front of Rosie, a lonely, beaten woman walked toward an empty apartment, while behind Rosie, stood a cherished collection, erected piece by piece—a monument to her large loving family.

- PART TWO -

Chapter 6

On a Tuesday, late afternoon, two weeks before the Christmas attack, Joe Fisher went to work just like any other day. He was tall, with a good build, curly black hair, and perpetual five o'clock shadow and a "rather be somewhere else attitude." Since leaving high school he'd been a janitor. Ten years before, Joe scored a well-paying position in New York City at the United Nations complex, mopping, sweeping, vacuuming, spraying and wiping. The routine days of tending to repetitive tasks reminded him of a laboratory rat running through an obstacle course, stopping here and there and sniffing, trying to get a small ration of oats.

My oats arrive every Friday. They come in the shape of a nice-looking piece of paper with numbers, a dollar sign, and a signature. Every year, a few more oats get dropped on the cage floor from the bosses upstairs. But it's a job, and it sure pays the bills.

This day, life chose to play a trick on him. Like the dutiful lab rat, he unknowingly acted out his role in the cosmic prank. Without seeing or considering a bigger picture, Joe's job responsibilities led him into the anonymous unknown. Up to that day, the "unknown" only happened to other people. TV shows, newscasts and the Internet told stories about such victims. He occasionally paid these some mind for the head-shaking, smirk-generating, entertainment value. "Gotta love them train wrecks!"

One routine task involved mopping the United Nations Archives Annex room, which also doubled as the Lost and Found. This lonely room was beneath the Secretariat Tower's 39 above ground floors and walled off from the underground parking. The

Lost and Found "department" is a metal rack with a half a dozen shelves. Each building in the UN complex had its own place for lost items.

On the concrete floor, Joe noticed a folded off-white cloth, hermetically sealed, in clear plastic. A mish-mash of items sparsely lay on the shelves: a child's sweater, the seasonal orphaned mittens, an emptied wallet and a few paperback and hardcover books, cell phones and car keys. "Jerks! How'd they drive home, huh!" He eyeballed the cloth. It didn't look like just another lost, yet to-be-found item.

Something was amiss. The sticker displaying the U.N.'s identification seal, stamped on an item's plastic bag during processing, had fallen off somewhere. Plus, the standard info tag was missing. The tag would have listed its date of receivership, location where it was found, identification of who found it, a description of the object and the employee who administered the labeling. Joe searched, but found nothing, except a floor needing a good brooming followed by a mop-up.

He looked at the thin cloth, probably folded at the time of its insertion into the plastic bag; roughly 5 by 10 inches of soft off-white fabric with a faint yellowish tint. Plus, ink markings of diagrams and words in a language foreign to him. Several small, light brown stains intermingled with the scribbles. He could see the edges of inner layers of the soft material. Fully unfolded, he figured, it would probably be six times its current size with the penned drawings and letters covering both sides.

He lost interest in what its markings might mean and muttered, "Hmm, okay. So, what to do with you my orphaned friend?"

It was his duty to take the item to the office of the building maintenance supervisor, John Stevens. That office was located one floor below. Stevens was a balding, clean-cut, graying , pot-bellied man. Good-humored, squat and surprisingly strong. He had a way of maneuvering conversations that caused most to respect and listen carefully to him. No one labeled him "wise," but that's what registered.

When Joe presented the curiosity, Stevens gave his opinion right away. "Nothing but a coffee stained napkin with fancy doodling on it. Somebody must be plannin' a war or somethin'."

Joe smirked. "That makes sense. Why didn't I think of that?"

Stevens pointed out a fancy embossed design running along the edges. He turned the napkin around, flipped it over and even held it close to a bright light examining the markings. He said, "So, this must have some important information on it, done during mealtime in the Delegates Dining Room by some smarty person or smarty persons plural," he added a self-satisfied snigger. "Perhaps a dignitary left this behind by accident or being not-so-important, meant to be laundered or thrown out as garbage with the leftovers. Obviously, the napkin is in the lost and found, all neat and tidy, as a courtesy to the dignitary or ambass-*odor*," he let out another snigger, "who might show up looking for it one day before we all die." Stevens further summarized, "This is a higher quality napkin than what's used upstairs. Why they brought it into the building is a mystery. Joe, I've seen plenty during my years here at the UN. And these right here are, high-class, professional doodles, m' man. Not your ordinary kind of ink scratches and scribbles, no siree. But, Joey m' boy, I figure these notes and sketches weren't designed to cause imminent global chaos, the total annihilation of the human race, or rock our nice, pleasant world. That is what my seasoned logic-based reasoning tells me."

Broom still in hand, Joe commented, "Well, boss, you can wipe your nose with it for all I care."

After a chuckle, John reminded Joe, "30 days is all we keeps 'em for. I'll date this little dude and contact someone and pass the buck." But John Stevens, who had worked at the UN far longer than Joe, figured the marked-up napkin was originally set aside for further review or study by one of the U.N. *shadows*. He figured somebody wanted to know exactly where it was and get it back pronto.

He added, "Our item of interest simply lost its way from point A to point B. Why it arrived unmarked and naked down here like this only shows that some jerk workin' ever so high above us slipped up and failed to do a proper job." In a voice right out of Dracula's Transylvania, and hands doing a peculiar unfolding and twisting, he added in a dead stare, "Let me remind you young Joey that international intrigue exists like an *invisible* web stretching from top to bottom in this skyscraper." A sardonic laugh followed.

Joe sneered and added a spooky, "Oh yeah! Come on and freak me out, baby!"

Chapter 7

The basement mop shop is located only one floor below the Archives Annex room. This grumbly bottom-feeder position in the United Nations food chain remained far in the back of Stevens' mind.

After the discussion with Joe, he notified the head of Archives about the anomaly. He liked using the word 'anomaly' just to sound intelligent to those higher-paid, highly-educated people who worked on the floors above him.

Elroy Hammond, Head of Archives Annex showed up at the mop shop. Stevens knew Hammond preferred the rarely used back stairs, instead of the long wait for an elevator ride of one floor filled with underground parkers.

The public rarely saw Mr. Hammond. So, he could wear a beard, shaggy hair, faded jeans, N.Y. Yankees ball cap and enjoyed an old sweater perpetually on the verge of all out tattering. His casual work uniform was bottom-offed by Birkenstock sandals and white socks. Round lenses in rimless glasses sat on his nose. As people go, he didn't mind working alone, but acted more like a reference librarian—just without any books to mother over.

Stevens, in a nonchalant manner, handed the clear package to Mr. Hammond.

Perplexed, he asked, "Mr. Stevens, where's the I.D. tag?" Still focused on the specimen, flipping it around and without looking at Stevens, his free hand reached outward in a gesture of expectation. Nothing landed there.

Stevens told the brief story, adding his own observations. With a chuckling New York accent, he said, "Hey! That's all I know, no tag, no got—so hey, sue me!"

Mr. Hammond winced at this attempt at humor, plus the jab at the mythical, well-oiled, record keeping machine of the United Nations.

"Mr. Stevens, don't worry. I won't be filing a lawsuit." Mr. Hammond's stiff vein of dry humor appeared lost on Stevens. Hammond said, "Tah, tah," and then returned one flight above—by the stairs.

When the office door closed, Stevens defined Elroy Hammond in one word, "Jerk!"

Mr. Hammond returned to his office with the package. He plunked down at his computer station while sipping lukewarm peppermint tea from his Yankee's mug. He attempted investigating which U.N. employees recently accessed the archives by the log book or requested materials. After creating a list, he emailed an inquiry. In the following hours, no one responded knowing anything about the lost, now found, napkin. Then, he contacted all U.N. eatery management staff at the Secretariat Tower, the entire custodial staff and shift managers in hopes of finding out which one turned in the item, or who might have spotted it.

After waiting two days, he huffed a sigh and scratched his head. "Wastin' my time on a silly whatever."

The expectations of the third day crawled by. Looking at his Inbox, Hammond rolled his eyes when useless replies and text messages stacked up. He clicked on each, sending them on their way to the lifeless Delete folder. Further perplexed about the object's origins, he searched the U.N.'s data base for possibilities. After another series of dead ends, Hammond figured he'd just officially place the napkin back in the lost and found and forget about it. In a flair of annoyance he reconsidered. With an odd, out-of-place item and no clues, he thought, *"What the hell, I'll just bug them upstairs one more time."* He wondered if the doodler simply didn't care that it was lost. Or worse, had reasons for embarrassment and secrecy. *Perhaps the odd document revealed private, personal or diplomatic secrets meant for no one to see. Or, maybe they want it back but, don't follow up on U.N. procedures. Or they don't read U.N. mass emails? Duh, I don't.*

Hammond grumbled about his 9-to-5 territory, a forgotten warehouse of the world in miniature. *"The United Nations serves a flexible number of member states—right now hovering at 190— besides pipsqueaks who consider themselves worthy of nation status. Each ambassador, dignitary and those in between networks a constant flow of trinkets, gifts and flowery cards or documents to other visiting or resident ambassadors. The clutter in most offices resembles a mini World Market import store in need of an emergency inventory reduction sale. That is, if there weren't a U.N. Archive Annex Department—or rather an international dump site… and me."*

He recited his cynical rip-off from the poem at the base of the Statue of Liberty.

"Give me what you are tired of,

Your poor, cluttered masses and growing piles,

You who are yearning to free up office space,

The wretched refuse of your teeming closets and bottom-drawers.

Send these to a new home, toss them to me, and then forget.

I lift my lamp to the shameless golden trash door!"

Hammond grunted and rolled his eyes. Rubbing his beard, he surmised *My professional expertise is… hmm, I've got it! Curator of the Unwanted and Orphaned. And Oh! The Globally Challenged.*

He took digital photos of the two visible sides of the napkin, still folded in the clear bag. He kicked himself for not doing this originally. With that addition, he emailed the same list of people and asked them to also forward this to anyone they knew, who might know something about the object. Appropriate security clearances were to remain intact.

In less than an hour, an email came back from far upstairs.

Hammond muttered. "How unusual. Now, it's wanted, weird."

The United Nations staffs a variety of linguists. Typically, they are CIA operatives with a minor in language and a major in international Peeping-Tommery. Some filled the ranks of the *shadows* who funneled intel back to D.C., Langley, somewhere in between, and places unknown.

The email came from Donald Griffin, a linguistics expert and head of the translation teams. He informed Hammond that a staff courier would be taking possession of the curious item from the archives department within the hour.

Moments later, a knock on his office door caught his attention. Opening the door, his demeanor brightened.

A young woman, who looked to be barely past her teens, stood level with him, with large and clear blue eyes. A pretty face and long curly light brown hair motivated him to glance lower. A slim body filled her tight-fitting U.N. uniform in all the right places, advertising an appealing figure. Elroy drank in her pretty smile, not passing up her cherry red lipstick. And he thought her name fit just fine too. Her badge read "Tiffany."

In a high-pitched feminine voice she said, "Hi, I'm Tiffany Reynolds. Mr. Griffin from Linguistics sent me to pick up a package that—" she looked at a small, hand-held, electronic device, "Elroy Hammond has in his possession. Can you help me mister...?"

The young lady's perfume had a radiating life of its own. When that filled his nostrils, this added to his stymied response. He halfway tried not to take further note of her looks, that is, until she took a cover-girl pose, pad in hand.

He gushed air and spoke like a man relieved of a forced strenuous exercise. "I, ahh… I'm the per-person you're looking for, Elroy, I mean, Mr. Elroy Hammond—that's me." He wondered if his fumbling voice and wide-eyed expression gave away his arousal. *I do work a lot of hours alone. I wish I was the something she had come for!*

Tiffany stepped closer and extended her electronic clipboard. "Then sign this please, Mr. Hammond," she said pointing to an X and thin line. She lightly tapped his shoulder with the stylus attached to the device.

Taking the stylus, he tried to remember his name. With annoyance, he stalled saying, "I, I ahh always hate these things; they're so clumsy. You can never see what you're writing and when you do, the signature…it's so distorted like I'm a three year-old with a crayon." He looked up at her, "Whatever happened to paper and pens, huh?"

She shook her head and tilted it to one side with a silly "Don't ask me!" look.

He squinted at her through his glasses. "By the way, Tiffany, this pick-up was kinda fast. I received notice of the transfer only a minute ago." He hoped for some explanation or clue to the napkin's owner and value.

She said with a wink. "Electronically too, I bet." He returned the clipboard, and for his complaints, only a slight grin appeared on her face.

They went to the small locker where Hammond had placed the cloth. Seeing the folded napkin through the plastic bag, Tiffany cheerily remarked, "Must be Jesus' napkin from the Last Supper or somethin'!"

Hammond grinned and let out a nervous chuckle; he liked a woman with quick wit. So he added, "I'm with you! But, the speed with which they wanted this thing upstairs makes me think it's more like a mini Shroud of Turin! Heh, heh." He whimsically rolled his eyes.

She held open a large manila envelope for him to place the bag in. With a mild "Hah!" and a broad grin she spun around on one foot and made for the door. Watching her every step, marked by a sexy wiggle, he succeeded in catching a memorable glance of her tightly-skirted rear end. When the door closed, he shook his head, smirked and smiled, *That was definitely the highlight of my day, and then some.*

Chapter 8

Early March. Three months after the attack.

With the hospital stay behind her, and after spending a restless week of boredom at home, Dr. Ryons returned to her job—and she was ready. Dr. Ryons emailed the lab from home, notifying the employees what day she would re-enter the workplace. The email did not contain anything of a personal nature. She clipped on her UNHQ photo identification security pass and walked out of her door. "Back to work and about damn time!"

She released her bodyguard, Bubba, even though he strongly desired to escort her in a taxi which he had arranged. The driver, Youssef, from Tunisia was a U.N. contact.

Rosie anticipated this departure and quickly went to the street entrance using the elevator. She cheerily handed out two bags of goodies. Lissa was pleased, but Bubba said that he wanted to throw Mrs. Roseblum over his shoulder and take her home with him.

*   *   *

A dim, rainy day greeted the still struggling survivor to the 18 acre complex. Strong winds blew in from the unforgiving Atlantic. Around the perimeter of the U.N. complex, soldiers with automatic weapons patrolled in pairs, some with guard dogs. *No wonder now why their uniforms are called fatigues.* Several blue helmets complimented the U.S. troops. She counted seven sand bagged machine gun nests partially covered due to the weather. A lone tank gave her no reassurance of safety. The U.S. military's presence shocked her. *Damn. Damn. Damn, serious alright! Working here will never be the same, never. And now it's lodged in my mind for good, too. Damn it all!*

Around the U.N. grounds, she noticed plenty of police in raincoats, on foot. *They're probably caught in a daily limbo of purpose; too late to have prevented the attack and too early to stop a potential future one. Thoughts and memories of 9/11 must be on their minds. No doubt each one of them is tough, tense, and not enjoying this chilly weather.*

Monday 8 a.m., her taxi stopped in front of her blasted home; the Secretariat Tower. For the first time, she saw the ugly, black maw of the shattered architecture. An immorally made, mouth-shaped opening. It appeared that the stunned building grieved, asking "Why?" in a perpetual, dreary groan, wrought from much pain. The horrible destruction, a broad half-circle, four stories high. After almost three months, Lissa could see only a little exterior rebuilding accomplished, surmising, *Government bureaucratic red tape, no doubt. Rolls 'n rolls of it.*

Construction workers with bright hard hats, and reflective orange vests, moved about on tiers of scaffolding, cranes and scissor lifts. Large swaths of thick clear plastic kept the weather out. A series of fluorescent orange caution cones and yards of yellow caution tape, met her eyes. She marveled at the influx of manpower. The presence of this crew of strangers inflamed her soul and seemed a violation of the door to her home.

Other emotions rose. Rethinking the gruesome night was unavoidable. She peered between the meandering rivulets on the taxi's windows and imagined the U.N. visitors and employees at the moment of the blast. Dread slowly weighed on her shoulders, her upper body sagged. Lissa's neck lost its strength. Pulled by gravity, a quivering chin met her heaving chest. Burying her face in the damp winter gloves, tears swelled and fell. Moans mixed with the aching sobs. *They found me on the ground over there, bloody and unconscious.*

When the taxi driver heard these sounds from the back seat, his head turned slightly. He didn't know what to do, so he waited. Given the lengthening seconds, waiting for this passenger to exit, the driver's awkwardness grew. Reckless violence was no stranger to him. This taxi driver emigrated from Libya to New York, less than five years before. He loved his new country.

The driver partially turned to face Lissa, silver tears running down his dark cheeks. Through choked sobs, his broken English and thick accent, he addressed his ride. Anger filling his heart, he vented his words in bursts, "Thees our hoem. Rrr home!" He raised his hands, fingers spread wide. "Thees d'stroyed! Ahgin, n' ahgin, thay 'tack us. Thay 'tac us all. Try thay doo ahgin…whant keel us. We dah gud peepul, u mee, gud."

Face still down, head nodding, Lissa reached for his shoulder and squeezed it. Her other hand located tissues in the purse. Blowing her nose, dabbing her cheeks, the moans slowed. Time passed. Shocked, she considered how her life almost ended here just a few feet away. The extra cost ticking away on the taxi's meter held no significance.

A rain-weary N.Y.C. policeman approached the car, two soldiers shadowing him.

He tapped the hood with his club, landing an authoritative thunk. In an impersonal, dictatorial tone he loudly pronounced, "If you have any official business here, its time to get out of the taxi and be ready to present your I.D. to me!" He waited a moment, then repeated the speech. His other hand inched closer to the snap on his holster. The officer moved to the driver's water-drenched window and peered in. He saw one white woman and one black man. Both were crying.

He froze.

After the U.N. reopened, during her absence, the lab crew operated satisfactorily without her leadership. Lars, who ranked next in seniority, ran it quite well.

During those weeks their roster included tasks sent from U.N duty stations in the field: tainted soil samples, explosives chemical residue, ballistics samples of ammunition trafficking, crop killing diseases, exhumed bodies and livestock maladies—the never ending bread and butter of forensic fare. Such investigative requests came from countries remaining unidentified due to U.N. lab protocols. This privacy and secrecy stunted potentially damaging or embarrassing rumors, and anonymous leaks to the media or by Internet postings. Projects used a mixed alphabet and number labeling system.

While riding up the elevator to her floor, tension in her crew climbed too. Throwing a party for their boss seemed out of place, yet the lab workers wanted to do something special—but didn't know what. So, upon her arrival they would do nothing. Thankfully, nothing was expected.

When she entered the lab, her frank, get-back-to-business attitude caused a collective sigh of relief. A simple "Welcome back!" and "Good to see you again, Doctor!" did the job. Her left arm in a sling, the many scabs and bruises were not mentioned. She found peace in that.

Dr. Ryons opened her office, the lights came on. The mini-blinds stayed shut and she closed the door. Her shoulders slumped. After exhaling a long breath which felt like she'd held in for two months, a grin broadened. *Home. I'm home.* It took quite an effort to get her lab coat on. She slid off her sling, pushed her braced wrist and sore arm through the lab coat sleeve and got the sling back on. The rest involved little struggling. "Ouches" and "Ows" didn't make it out past her office enclosure.

Her body arched backwards a little—because the fragrance from a bouquet of flowers filled the small room. Before looking at the card she placed her bruised face and medicated head into the small forest of beauty. "Flowers! Ahh…just what I needed."

Dr. Ryons opened the envelope which advertised the United Nations Floral Gift Shop. Inside was a generic, "Glad You're Back. Get Well Soon!" greeting card. This item, she knew to be a stock card by the imprint of the famed U.N. building, with flags flying, iconic olive branch seal, plus title and name of the serving Secretary General. She started to read a printed info-caption. *"Daily, almost 200 flags fly here…"* She set it down. *Yeah? I'm not too impressed right now.*

This timely gift arrived at the direction of someone whose job it is to be in-the-know. No doubt that person worked in the H.R. department. A "Thank you!" card or chocolates to a certain ambassador, a card and popular toy for someone's child going in for surgery or "Congratulations!" when an employee had a baby. All were the same—no handwritten signatures, only mass produced facsimiles. Flower arrangements found their way to any floor, to those needing a beautiful perk—bombing victims included.

"One more." She glanced at the card, then reached for the waste basket. *"…each of the current 179 flags are hoisted and lowered…."* She hesitated, but let the impersonal sentiments drop and returned to the bountiful bouquet. She grinned, plowing her face into the colorful oasis, a paradise in her office. Penetrating deep into her core flourished an absorbing appreciation. Every vibrant color, every perfect petal and separate fragrance literally washed away years of something within her that had stagnated and mutated, atrophying to no use. Such a place, where what made her unique as a woman, now regained its fertileness.

Feeling like a child at a memorable birthday party, exhilaration filled her. Lissa moved the flowers closer. She wanted to keep inhaling the blending fragrances. With a quick pluck, she pulled out a single red carnation. In a one-handed effort, she cut the stem short and pushed it through her lab coat button hole. In this brief glinting addition, there emerged a transitioned, improved Lissa Ryons. Through the rest of the day whenever she eyed the bouquet, a bright flair of emotion washed through her.

Each day after this, Dr. Ryons wore a flower. Though done by rote, and slightly tethered to something else, a facet of grandeur always ornamented her. After several days, when the bouquet's conscripts wilted, she decided to have the floral gift shop send up a fresh blossom each morning. Her email stated, "Any flower will do."

The significance of the floral addition to her appearance never quite registered in her conscious mind. After securing the flower, her heart moved on in a blink. No grin, no smile remained. Also, she didn't feel like the special someone of someone special. No, that special place in her feminine heart had dried up. Such appreciations of romance ended long ago. An image flashed in her imagination. She sat on a bed in a darkened room; the silhouette of a man in the doorway, leaving forever. Another image followed. She stood over an open toilet, as the water flushed she tossed a diamond ring. These memories rose and vanished before her heart caught up with the pain cinched to it.

The ongoing beauty and promise of a new day's blossom of brilliant color did not parallel what churned deep in her soul. Each morning when Dr. Ryons attached a new blossom, a spurt of delight well-up, but fast as a shooting star, the feeling went far and shone no more. This juxtaposition was as if she had placed the fresh flower on a cold, sterile, metallic specimen tray and shelved it. The two did not match; wearer and worn. Only on the surface did viewers misconstrue this bonding. When a lapelled flower generated a compliment or smile, nothing registered in Lissa. She ignored them all. Passivity won out.

Snipped at dawn from a living plant, the petals burst with vivid hues. Purchased for public exposure in a button hole meant a clicking time clock of life. Superseded by wilting and withering, followed by certain death, rejection, and the inevitable disposal in a trash bin. Lissa lived in a cloudless, starless twilight, and she knew it well. A lovely sunset never preceded the coming darkness of her night.

Chapter 9

Settling in to her office, Dr. Ryons spent hours cleaning out her email inbox. This included e-cards from her four grandchildren whom she had only seen in photos. Well-wishing emails from colleagues and some from U.N. employees whom she could not place. *Trying to care, I guess*, she mused and bit her lip. The automated corporate sympathy e-cards just annoyed her. She found clearing out and ferreting the spam email a profound pain to her sanity. *No Viagra for me today… sure of that!*

Due to the sling and wrist brace she typed with the one good hand, but occasionally in a wily fashion, she managed to peck from her restrained sore hand. Ryons did her best to reply to necessary correspondences. She ordered her favorite herbal tea drink from the espresso bar on the main floor. The Chamomile Shuffle arrived free of charge, as a 'welcome back' to a regular customer. The smiling delivery girl also bestowed a free single drink certificate to her. Then she asked for Dr. Ryons' punch card and punched two holes.

Back to the computer, drink on her desk. Though unnecessary, but with a perfectionist's drive, she read every report her crew produced during her absence. *Lars did an excellent job.* Yet, this complimentary truth never made it from her mind to his ears.

Dr. Ryons shoved one stack of papers aside, and a fine white feather several inches long wafted into the air. This unexpected visitor spun once and lay down. She wondered how the oddity entered her office. Picking it up by the point she twirled the mystery between her thumb and index finger. *Pigeon? Dove?* She pried apart two mini-blinds to look through her office window wondering which one of the crew left it, and why. After curious possible meanings evaporated, she held the feather over the trash can. But on a whim, she changed her mind, set the feather in the top desk drawer and closed it.

A less imposing pile of paper mail awaited her, such as fresh documents requiring her signature. Besides the business at hand, returning a lengthy list of phone calls entailed trudging through inquiries as to her 'health' and remarks concerning the tragedy. Each sympathetic segment of a conversation sounded to her like the previous one. She raced through every get well card and then disposed them all. *That's irritating! I don't have any use for generic sympathy or encouragement. Please! If there were only some way to bottle that up and sell it, I could make a fortune in the grief industry marketing kind words spoken in just the right way. A little is way more than I need! Enough is enough. Can't we just talk about work and our duties at hand, please!*

By unnecessary, yet unstoppable meticulousness, three days later Ryons finished her office tasks. She nearly shouted, "Finally, I can get back to a normal routine!" Returning to her job definitely helped speed up her healing. Dr. Ryons had returned home.

* * *

Since she ran lead on the napkin research before the terrorist attack, her team kept the item in its secure drawer and assumed other duties. The Linguistics Department seemed to have dropped interest in it after the Christmas Bombing. During her last days before release from the hospital, Ryons daydreamed on her bed, intent on discovering the odd properties of the visiting napkin. Now that she was back, the scientist sought to implement these ideas.

At first opportunity, she opened the drawer, scissors in hand, and stared. Silence. The napkin didn't communicate any recognition of her. No pulse of light, no shimmer, marking her return. Way back, far in the darkness of her heart, the idea of friendship caused a spark. Dr. Ryons looked sideways to see who was watching—no one. She let out a huff of air and carefully severed the corners of the napkin. Each one inch triangle bore a small amount of the dark blue ink, used for the strange language.

The U.N.s typical out-sources testing—four university laboratories—would receive a sample. Forensics had used the same universities for years. The research goals? Approximate a date for the napkin and analyze the chemical compound of the fabric and ink.

Dr. Ryons preferred using a standard, blind study method. This meant a contracted third party kept the customer's name, occupation and purposes, private.

She chose to leave out the cloth's unusual characteristics of self-luminosity and study that on her own. *If the other labs find it, they're welcome to run with it.* When time allowed, she poured her curiosity through a sieve of scientific expertise.

Her lab's current roster included colorful international incidents and crimes. Such as, deliberate polluting of certain water tables of a third world country; airborne carcinogenic gases, identifying ammunition residue in order to trace supply lines used in more than one assassination attempt; the effect of recent volcanic eruptions on the ozone layer; and finally, investigating claims of unlawful genetic research on sex trade workers in a Latin American country.

The crew members didn't follow international news— current events came along with their shrouded project requests. Disarmament, peacekeeping, challenges such as hunger, natural disasters or diseases—these controversies overwhelmed. Bad news headed their way, in the front door and back out the same. Their job did not include learning the names of the dead or seeing that justice was done. They provided technical assistance and scientific expertise, advice and guidance for field offices. International tragedies and occasional preventative measures kept their lab the sick bay for the ills of over 175 nations. Every continent had member states who wanted to utilize whatever resources the United Nations offered. Membership fees were on a sliding scale, of course. The crew often emailed and Skyped with other U.N. employees around the globe.

Ryons glumness and brooding came and went as the days passed. Twice a week physical therapy appointments made her feel like a helpless steak repeatedly grilled on both sides. But the magic napkin simmered on the back of her mind and vied for position at the forefront of her bruised skull.

Before the attack. December 8

Mr. Donald Griffin, head of Linguistics, checked the sealed napkin. Then he replaced the item and added paperwork to the manila envelope. He bounced that further upstairs to the forensics team for inspection and safety analysis.

When Tiffany arrived with the transfer to Forensics, a lab worker signed and then handed it to Dr. Ryons. She read the sparse information within the envelope, which aroused her curiosity. When she slid the item out of the envelope, one nearby lab tech said, "A marked-up napkin? C'mon Doc, don't we have some real work to do around here?" He held up the specimen and turned to the others at their work stations. He spoke in a loud snooty voice, "Any bets on how long this'll be active for us? I say it's in the trash before the weekend."

A running bet sprang up decreeing that the napkin would end up in the garbage, at the latest, by the week's end. Since this was a Monday, exactly how many days such a trashing would take, became the crew's real brain teaser. A dry erase board showed the names and guesses jotted down. Dr. Ryons declined.

She intervened into the banter and asserted, "Even the plans for the first voyage to the moon probably started on a harmless, insignificant napkin like this. Let's give it a little respect, people." This dulled the brief light-hearted atmosphere.

Doctor Ryons treated the contents of the bag as possibly containing hazardous substances and entered the examination room dressed for the procedure. The cloth rested in an airtight, glass containment cell on a stainless steel table. She reached her hands into the fixed rubber sleeves and maneuvered the precision robotic arms to grip the plastic bag. Then she utilized a cutting tool to snip the bag open and carefully removed the cloth with tongs, laying it folded flat. On her nod, one of the assistants pressed a variety of buttons on a console to start the chemical scanning process. An overhead video camera recorded the entire procedure.

One of the crew melodramatically volunteered, "That left-over laundry detergent can be a killer! Stand b-b-b-back everyone!"

Appropriate snickers followed. Lars raised his arms in mock alarm.

Eyes rolling, Lissa's head see-sawed, "Yeah, yeah. Lethal."

Within minutes, tiny green lights on an array of computers coincided with high-pitched beeps. Graphs on the screens and accompanying readouts revealed mundane results. Tests showed no trace elements of anything dangerous or suspicious.

Lissa opened the containment cell's lid with gloved hands and made a home for the napkin on a large metal tray. Unfolded, the material measured 16 by 30 inches. An odd aroma wafted up from the fully opened, freed cloth. Dr. Ryons inhaled, breathing deeply through her nose. Her face brightened. Then the crew of four assistants silently circled the napkin, breathed in and commented on a pleasing fragrance.

One twitched his nose, "Smells like perfume my mother used to wear." He paused, retained a sniffle and added, "I do miss her." Each in turn leaned in to sniff, and then get an even better whiff. "Reminds me of roses and anniversaries." Another said, "No, I think it's the ocean, near the tropics. Lyin' on the beach and lovin' it!" The only female assistant, named Marge, short for Marjorie, interjected, "You're all wrong. It's a warm, rain forest, moist and green with adventure. I swear I can hear parrots!"

Chuckles followed that exaggeration.

Smiling to herself, Lissa quietly said, "Chamomile." Just above a whisper, with slumped shoulders she added for no one's ears, "Calms me down."

After inhaling the passing curiosity and no need to accurately determine the fragrance, all of the assistants moved back to work.

Using tongs, Dr. Ryons weighed the corners to stretch the visiting cloth tight. She motioned for Lars to photograph each side. For lab records she noted the dark blue penned language and various colors for the designs and diagrams.

Before the end of the day, the napkin entered a new zip lock plastic bag, and then another United Nations Forensics Department manila envelope. The photographs burned to a disc, plus printouts of the instruments' findings were also included. One of the crew cleaned off the dry-erase board. No winners.

Chapter 10

December 9

The Linguistics department received an email from Forensics, and the package arrived back at Griffin's desk, once again via Tiffany.

On the next day his team reviewed the lab results. One week later, a meeting took place. Mr. Donald Griffin—part interrogator, larger part security and small part "linguist"—was leading it, and leading it nowhere.

Don Griffin worked a significantly well-salaried position which any number of more deserving persons failed to be chosen for. So, why was his name on the door? Simply put, he had connections. He was head of the U.N. *shadows.*

He was in his late 40s and engaged in fighting off the idea that he lived on the older side of being young. In the mirror, every morning, his balding hair told him different. He could be seen walking down the Secretariat Tower halls with his shirt not fully tucked in; food particles on his mustache, which needed a good trimming; his tie looking as if he knotted it in the dark and remnants of breakfast or lunch stains on his suit. Griffin never noticed his unkemptness. Mrs. Griffin and their children had given up tending to his appearance years ago. Because of his careless or blind behavior, they asked and expected little from him—for reasons he never pondered. No one liked him, or his looks, or cared for his domineering, hothead leadership.

Griffin had no interest in making friends with his coworkers. He wasn't bothered by the friendships and camaraderie others around him enjoyed. Without too much scratching of his head, he'd dismissed the entire idea of friendship years ago. Really, he hadn't made the genuine efforts needed to be a friend. If personalities could have a limp, his did.

At the meeting he spoke to a dozen men and women. He emphatically stated, "No paperwork! No records of any type! Nothing in the system! No surveillance footage in the hallways! Only fingerprints from the two janitor types and that hippie in the basement. Tiffany knew better, being dainty, as only that young woman can. She merely pinched the top of the manila envelope while in transit."

Griffin's briefing continued. Yet, after forty-five minutes, they sat puzzled staring at looping photos on a large plasma screen in the conference room. The computer-enhanced lettering and designs zoomed in and out, spun around, appeared X-rayed, pixilated and colored differently. Each participant clicked the same files on their laptops, having received them several days ago when the investigative efforts commenced.

Annoyed at his underlings, a favorite perk of his job, Griffin complained. "You're the top U.N. linguistics team. But after one week you've given me nothing but silly suggestions, blank stares, and promises to re-research online and offline publications … as if I didn't know the drill. I haven't even heard one fully crazy conspiracy theory! Maybe I should take you to a few grungy subway stations to hear really creative ideas for free, huh?"

Knowing many of his team had Christmas shopping on their minds, Griffin upped the ante. "The traffic on terrorist websites and intercepts by agents in the field talk about attacks intent on disrupting New York's Christmas shopping or worse—destruction of landmarks. Yes, I know it's an annual bogey boys and girls. But, this nap-kinny document has no birth record, blood type, parents or lineage, if you catch what I mean. But somehow it came under our roof!" He flailed his arms, "I'm spooked. I want you spooked. So, get your spook on!"

With a raised voice, he nearly shouted again, "Decode the damn bastard, ASAP! For now, send the specimen back to Forensics for advanced testing and a secure resting place.

December 17

Tiffany returned the specimen the following day. When the cloth arrived, and paperwork organized, Dr. Ryons had the napkin placed in an "Inactive" cabinet drawer in the back of the lab.

"When you have valid ideas, something worth my time to look at, I'll take a break from sipping hot spiced apple cider. I want to see what you're getting paid for." Conniving, he joked, "I am officially out-of-the-loop! That is, of course, until after the holidays. I must devote myself to spreading holiday cheer. Santa, bring it on. I'm ready! You elves get to work."

He left the meeting smug and smiling. Shopping for cheap, nominal gifts that would satisfy his family lay heavy on his mind.

For fear of a worse exhibition of his temper and lost holiday overtime, the team threw together not-so- new clever guesses, complete with Internet images, near meaningless colorful graphs and then copied and pasted online textbook theories they hoped would be beyond the boss' comprehension. They also mixed in reworded, previous conclusions with a twist. At times like these, such productions, made to look above his intelligence level, turned into a secret game which the team played behind his back.

The elves' work arrived on Griffin's desk at the end of the following day. The team smirked with pride at the wondrously worded and illustrated report, trusting their efforts to have made it impossible for the boss to tell how little it varied from what they had presented the day before. They were a demotivated, but gifted crew, working for a man harnessing less brains than any one of them, yet harvesting a bigger crop on payday.

This exhibition of speed under pressure truly impressed their leader. Liking what he read, as an added layer of security, Griffin emailed the team, with orders directing them to send any further findings strictly to him. After studying the latest guesswork, he made a few phone calls and forwarded the findings to an off-site government headquarters. In a few days, analysts gleaned a strange thread which required another attempt to retrace the finding of the curious cloth.

December 20

In return, Griffin received orders which surprised him. He made plans for a meeting of a different sort, coordinating with an outside crew used for special operations. The following day this tight, solemn group took the elevator down as far as it went, for an appointment with an employee Griffin had never met before, Joe Fisher, a janitor.

Chapter 11

December 21

Once Joe received the text message to report "immediately," he headed to John Steven's office.

Typically, when the small army of janitors arrived for work they checked clipboards for their assigned tasks. These to-do lists hung on the wall outside of the office. Stevens and his crew communicated with walkie-talkies and cell phones for questions, conflicts, or revised instructions. Two weeks had passed since Joe Fisher picked up a linen napkin from the floor at the lost and found. He'd never thought of it since.

Joe rarely saw the inside of his boss's office. The exception was the crowded annual Winter Break party, previously called the Christmas party. Dozens of maintenance workers crammed into the office for cheap punch and cookies, and BS'ed about work or sports. But now as he entered, several U.N. officials stood, staring at him. Three were the nameless suits whose offices he perpetually cleaned and straightened after they left for the day. Two large surprise visitors held the door open for him—armed security guards. Each man wore an earpiece with a coiled wire leading into their clothing. He was shocked when they patted him down and pointed to a chair. They clasped their hands at their waists and stood motionless on either side of him, eyes straight ahead.

Then Stevens got up and left his chair to step out for a "break" following a suggestion by one of the anonymous suits. With mixed emotions and aimless suspicions, he glanced at Joe and left. He didn't like this at all. He especially didn't like his office invaded, without knowing why. Plus, he considered Joe a good kid, somewhat grumpy, but did his work well, and on time.

After the door clicked closed silence took over the room. Once the suits let the privacy and isolation settle in, their questions commenced. Without any introduction, a man pressed him with, "Mr. Fisher, how did you get access to the secure U.N. seal making machine?"

Joe looked at the faces and his feelings of bewilderment and awkwardness grew while thoughts of innocence took a defensive stance.

A deep voice asked, "Mr. Fisher, how did you know how to operate the hermetic fastening device? Who's working with you?"

Another said, "Fisher, do you have any formal training in ordnance construction, fine art, astronomy or astrophysics that you didn't include on your job app ten years ago? What foreign languages do you know? If you volunteer information now, it may make the going easier if or when we press charges!"

An unfriendly voice right behind his head spoke with accusation, "Do you like your job?"

Joe squinted in disgust and half-turned. "Whaa? What kinda question is that?"

Finally, penetrating his confused mind like a sharp rap on the top of his head, he heard, "Fisher, are you part of an extremist religious group intent upon overthrowing modern society as we know it? Any affiliation with hate groups? We will find out, so tell us now!"

Joe's movements to look at each investigator and this bam-bam-bam pressurized interrogation almost spun him off his seat. Disoriented, he gazed in unbelief at the questioners and the security guards who remained stiff and silent.

Then, all the suits bent slightly forward waiting for him to answer.

This unexpected confinement caused every inch of his skin to redden and rise in temperature. He raced to sort out possible answers to these outrageous accusations. He came up with none, and looked empty and vacant. A compounding queasiness made the inner free fall worsen.

Inside, Joe turned into an untamable whirlwind. Mentally, he lost control—up, down, twisting and contorting, he spun like an electric blender switched to "Emotions on High." He tried to calm himself. But, there was no "STOP" button to be found. *It's okay. Just get up and walk out the door and go back to work … these men will not follow you!* He felt caged in by fools with firearms. *Highly-paid fools with firearms.*

The janitor had no answers and stared as blank as the bare cement floor before him. What could he say? All he knew were dirty floors, brooms, squirt bottles and rags. Someone shoved him. Then he heard a firm, authoritative voice order to "stand down." He heard some murmuring about lawyers and protocols from voices that seemed to come from the floor and at the same time from above his head and around the room. *Scary, very scary. This ain't April Fools' Day … no, this is a day in late December!*

Joe slowly raised his head, looking for the probable one in charge. *But, in charge of what?* He spoke in a sluggish, waking kind of voice, "Ultra, what?" His bright red face and accumulating sweat didn't help.

Perplexed at this question, the men looked at each other. Pushed with annoyance, one voice pronounced, "What? No one said, 'ultra' anything!"

Joe tried to read the man's name tag. It appeared to be a miscellaneous assortment of letters. *Grif' something.* It slid down into the bottomless hole of shifting, changing faces of dignitaries and ambassadors and staff who he passed by every day on the job.

"You asked or mistook me to be a member of an ultra religious group or something."

With a stern voice, the man replied, "Don't put words in our mouths! Messing with us, buddy, that's the last thing you want to do right now! We said 'extremist religious group' but 'ultra' will do, if that's a confession from you."

The questioning and accusations continued in a lingering nightmare for an hour or two. Joe didn't want to ask for a lawyer because he wanted to leave the room with his employment intact. So, he put the lawyer-being-present-thing out of his mind. He hoped the inquisition would stop, and soon. Much to his disappointment, the latter didn't come soon enough. Joe didn't know what they were talking about and more importantly it didn't seem that they knew what they were talking about. *With these guys, if I ask for a lawyer it means I'm guilty.* With a spark of reality through half-closed eyes he pondered, *After all, I'm not being arrested… am I?*

Through clenched teeth, he flatly asked, "Am I under arrest, because I want to go now?"

This worried the suits. They decided they'd better try a nice approach and see if that got him talking. "Look, we're all getting tired and hungry, Joe." A faked perky voice added. "What kinda toppings you want, on ahh pizza, whatever yah want? A.S.A.P. Maybe a beer or two will clear things up, huh? Hey! Then we can all go home. Yeah." Grunts and feigned, "Sure." and "Hey! Good idea," rotated around the room.

Joe mumbled off a few inconsequential toppings from his bruised mind.

When the food arrived from the U.N. commissary he barely ate a slice and only sipped his bottle of beer.

The other men talked up how good it all tasted and appeared thankful for the break. For them, chewing broke the fruitless tedium.

The meal only compounded how reckless and full-of-it he felt. *Prisoner in a cage? No!* He slammed the bottle down and threw his slice back into the box. Before his mind overloaded he lashed out. "Leave me alone. I'm just a grunt…a regular guy around here. I don't know nuthin.' I haven't got no idea what you're talkin' about. You got the wrong guy, you jerks!" These were his last words at the miserable meeting. He stood up, and with unfocused vision brushed passed the suits and security guards. Uncertain of what to do, they parted for him. His head and mind ached. Now he really wanted a beer.

Chapter 12

December 24

Joe the janitor found a note on his clipboard from the supervisor to come in the office. He went inside and exchanged greetings with Stevens. Waiting for him, on his boss' desk, Joe found a sealed U.N. envelope. Stevens handed it to him, then pretended to shuffle paperwork on his desk, waiting for Joe's reaction.

Joe ripped open the envelope. In the enclosed print out, a mere typed paragraph explained that previous to his interrogation, labeled as "questioning," government authorities intercepted a bomb threat on the Internet, directed at the United Nations. The unmarked, sealed napkin Joe innocently turned in, appeared "suspicious in nature, containing diagrams of known bomb-making apparatus, and a style of coded language which secretive terror cells use." No apology of any sort. Then, an early Winter Break bonus caught his eyes, which, in his quick estimation, amounted to at least three times that of last year's check. He muttered, "Weird."

After noticing something else in the envelope, he shook his head several times, saying, "Those bastards! Those damn bastards!" Enclosed, he found several gift certificates for four large pizzas plus beverages at the commissary. With bitter thoughts, Joe let these fall on Stevens' desk.

The boss stopped pretending and he looked at the certificates and then stared up. Joe stomped out of the office, check in hand. Stevens heard a grumpy voice proclaim, "Merry Christmas boss, eat up!"

Chapter 13

Before the attack. December 24

At 5p.m., her crew gone home, Dr. Lissa Ryons smiled. *Alone in my lab.* She enjoyed this time the most, for the lab was her real home. As a professional she wasn't embarrassed to think of it that way. She puttered about in her white lab coat, finding small things to keep herself busy. After so many years in a sterile work environment, this transitioned into first nature to her. The other home was where she went later in the night and slept in a perpetually unmade bed. Dirty dishes and piles of assorted, unwanted snail mail grew by the day. She found satisfaction in occasionally tidying up the apartment, but since nobody visited her, why the effort?

At the lab, Dr. Ryons was different. She made stacks of paper rigidly square, placed pencils and pens parallel to each other, found an instrument or two which hadn't been returned to their proper drawer and did so in square alignment. She inspected all laboratory cabinets and drawers with a purpose of correcting the incorrect. She enjoyed knowing that each morning she would find the lab exactly as she left it. *I'm simply thorough,* she told herself. Deep within, she wanted notice and praise for these small activities. Her mind didn't think so, yet in her heart Lissa yearned for completion of loose ends—emotional ones, too. This prevailing of completing or inventing trivial tasks, night after night, indicated such want, which she had no conscious awareness of. She even came in on Saturdays for a few hours, alone. Pride in her dedication clouded the truth of this isolation eating one more day away to nothing.

The lab crew assumed that the night janitor did his or her job exceedingly well. Though in their minds—where unconnected thoughts simmered, the crew knew that no janitor would have done so much—this quality went beyond mopping and scrubbing. No one conceived that their boss stayed late every night doing this anal routine. None wanted to believe that she was fastidious.

At 7:30 p.m., Dr. Ryons finished answering stray email and poking around the Internet at science news websites. She double-checked the individual laboratory stations and readied herself to go home. After switching off all the interior lights, she noticed a glow at the far end of the lab. Thinking it must be a small desk lamp she missed, she went there slowly walking in the dark.

"Now this is wrong! What the…?" A specimen lay on a metal tray. "The doodled-up napkin. I haven't seen that out since Griffin sent it back on the 17th. I know I didn't see it out earlier today."

A yellow radiance illuminated the cloth and blurred the fine hemmed edges—now tinged with a bluish glow. If she could have seen herself, the reflected color made her face look beautiful. *The light coming from the far end of the lab was the napkin? No way! This was not in the report! And why didn't the scans detect the phosphorescence?*

Then the uniqueness of what was happening captivated her. *Why does the damn thing have luminescence? Does it glow during the day but we didn't notice? Or does it gather light during the day and reveal this characteristic in darkness? We never put it in an unlit room during work hours. Can it generate light independently?*

Then, she did something only children do when face to face with the unwelcomed unknown. "Not scientific, but what the hell, I'm alone!" She closed her eyes, waited a moment and reopened them. "Still there. Hmm. Just what are you?"

Eeriness caused her to catch her breath. Surprise overtook her and darkness surrounded the faint scene. The lone scientist moved closer to the napkin. Her mind lost its momentum and stopped thinking. The analytical doctor diminished; womanly instinct rose to the surface and took over.

Extending her fingers to the anomaly, she pinched a corner of the napkin and then gently rubbed. A pleasant, slight surge of power moved into her fingertips, filled her palm, and rose up past the wrist. She sighed as emotions swelled and Lissa found herself valuing an unexpected peace. No opinions, no questioning or resistance, merely a pleasing sensation. Her shoulders relaxed, lowered and rounded; arms hung loose. She exhaled. Head nodded low, breaths settled, in and out, in a relaxed rhythm. Time slowed and then stood still, a tonic to her soul.

She grinned, *I feel good,* and closed her eyes. For how long she didn't know. After her rest, slow lids opened. Then, the color, designs and diagrams appeared to lift off the cloth and circulate like blood traveling through veins. The dark blue lettering swam too. The cloth become canvas, a place mat—no, a screen for a flicked on miniature neon world filled with life—a show! Intriguing ideas rushed into her imagination. Multiple schematics and intricate, designs lay fascinating yet indiscernible to her. No moment in her life surpassed this flurry. Her intelligence functioned fully with her heart tracking by its side. *These are plans. No wonder we conducted tests. But, plans for what?*

Then, she opened her fingertips and let go of the corner of the cloth—later, she wondered 10,000 times, *Why did I let go?* For now the curious, esoteric purposes lasted as only fragmented, vague mysteries. The images on the cloth returned to their previous state, the movement and vibrancy gone. She wasn't sure, but Lissa pondered, *Did I just bond with it, with that?* She shivered at her shoulders and then the internal commotion raced downward to her toes. Clarity drifted and slowly returned from these deep-roaming thoughts which had all lumbered to an unreachable mental location of the lost and forgotten. Months later, she would call them 'inspired.' In those days ahead she'd find herself scribbling 'Inspired' on Post It notes and most any piece of paper or napkin her hand rested on. Employees working with her learned to ignore this odd habit. They presumed residual brain damage caused involuntary glitches of behavior and this was one to ignore.

After Lissa, the female, let go, Dr. Ryons, the scientist returned. She took two steps back. But she hesitantly reached for the cloth, then stopped. Drawing back her poised arm, she corrected herself, *This is not proper lab procedure, what am I doing?*

Whatever just happened, the curious researcher experienced enough for one night. Dr. Ryons was torn between putting her lab coat back on, conducting experiments, running tests and researching the napkin on the Internet, or simply going home. But, no. Waiting until tomorrow made the most sense. Logically, she'd have the crew help her probe the possibilities. *Finding answers could wait until tomorrow… surely.* She put the tray with the specimen back into the drawer. The peace which came from briefly touching the cloth had subdued some of that investigative drive; but she did not realize this.

The scientist's sterile home had an intruder, and she deferred to it.

At the door, Dr. Ryons glanced backwards and walked out. In the hallway she locked the door and checked a second time to be sure it was really locked—not wanting "it" to walk away during the night. She left slightly befuddled, accompanied by a growing and absorbing inquisitiveness which she had not felt for years. She pondered going back to the lab and peeking in. *Just to see.* But no.

She considered a story from years ago, when her life was not good. A flicker of that memory roused a peculiar smile, as she muttered "Strange Cargo."

* * *

Walking down the hall toward the elevator, Dr. Ryons mentally wandered through an expanding corridor of thought moving along a hall of wonder lit by everyday fluorescent lights. One side contained life as she had always known it; the other held the unknown, like a cloudy gray fog. Concentration totally absorbed every second, every breath. Ryons thought it peculiar that she kept stepping on the very ideas and bizarre concepts she hoped to avoid. In order not to slip and fall out of her reality, the doctor told herself, the next day's investigation would surely solve the mystery. How pleasant the emotional stimulus had kicked her brain into high-gear. *Or, would it? Would the unknown vanish giving way to logic? Of course it would.*

Her mind involuntarily functioned as holding tank, a laboratory of deep thoughts ... thoughts she never expected to consider. What had occurred behind that locked door, coupled intense curiosity with a queasy insecurity. This made her sidle along.

At the elevator she pressed the button, put on her winter coat zipped it, slipped on her gloves, then positioned her purse and waited.

At that moment, Dr. Ryons wanted listening ears, and yearned for an audience of any sort—maybe the people in the elevator? But impulsively blurting out a spasm of strange facts to an impromptu group would only peg her as a weirdo loose in the building. She couldn't tell strangers any of this. She held a unique secret and stood enmeshed in it and alone.

Involuntarily, her mind rehearsed a speech for the ride down with a car of passengers. *Hello everyone! I know you don't know me and you only want to continue your trip to whatever floors you have chosen, but I have something important to share. This won't take long, so please*

76

don't press the emergency button or think I have a weapon. Would one of you kindly press the STOP button? In her mind, someone would.

I am Dr. Lissa Ryons and I work here at the United Nations in the Forensics Laboratory. A moment ago something really special happened which I think would fascinate every one of you or... actually anyone. That's why I want you to listen to what I have to say. I will be as quick as I can. Here it goes.

My department received a misplaced napkin. Oh, that sounds stupid! Let me start again. A napkin with really interesting sketches and a strange language written on it came to our lab from the lost and found—that's in the basement, by the way. Oh, that part sounds silly, too. Anyway this napkin, it's the thick cloth kind, not paper, and not one with the UN embossing either. Well, like I said, it has odd writings and diagrams on both sides. They're really perplexing. No one knows who made it. The person would be great to find—boy, I'd really love to meet whoever it is, especially after what just happened. I know, I know, I'm getting to that part.

My crew ran the cloth through various tests; the typical kind—don't worry, I won't bore you. Off the record, nothing unusual resulted. But, get this! A few short moments ago when I was closing up—something changed. Yes, I know it's after hours—but I'm not a workaholic. Nope, not me.

At this point, Dr. Ryons imagined the small, boxed-in, captive audience leaning in. "Yes, go ahead. Please, tell us!" All faces had expressions of anticipation, eyes wide open.

Are you all with me? Not waiting for an answer, she would continue in a hurried voice.

Tonight, just like every night, being the last to leave, I turned off all the lights in the lab. Then it happened. I noticed a light in the back. When I went to see what it was, guess what I found? The source was the napkin! Yes, that scribbled-up napkin! The cloth and the doodles—

well, that's what we've referenced them as, 'doodles.' I know that's not much of a technical term, but it works. The specimen glowed! That's not supposed to happen. I mean, do your napkins glow? Probably not. What a crazy surprise, huh? Then the ink came alive racing around. Talk about dazzling! I stared, shocked at my discovery.

Barely containing her enthusiasm, she'd emphasize in a confiding tone, *You folks are the first to hear about this. I'm almost done. A few more facts and then I'm finished, I swear. Just hold on, please.*

Then, I crept right up to the specimen and touched it. I wasn't in danger; well, I guessed that I wasn't. No, I didn't fall on the floor, flop around or begin to glow either. But guess what? I felt good. Here she'd look down and when she lifted her head Lissa had blushed sharing this intimate, private fact.

I felt good. She paused in her rambling and meditated on that fact a long moment.

Let me back up. A surge entered my fingertips and filled me. A surge. Like an increased awareness of things I enjoy, but weren't there. I mean, I love flowers. I realized how much I really do love flowers and need more of them in my life. This set in motion a whole series of emotions because of my appreciating this or that. In an exciting rush, I remembered so many things I'd forgotten. All of this happened in only a matter of moments. I know that couldn't be, but I checked my watch. You know how a download contains so much complicated data but it does so in seconds—kind of like that.

I felt a strengthening power, a warmth or force. I liked it. You would've too, I'm sure, yes, I'm sure. I know I'm talking a mile a minute. I just want to get it all out and you're all being so patient!

So, either these feelings just came into me, or the surge made my own feelings become wildly stronger, livelier. Either way, it caused a change in me. And, I ahh…I mean, I well…I felt good about myself. I liked me. I haven't felt like this for a long time. I know that's kinda...weird and personal stuff. Yeah, believe me, boy do I know.

In her daydream, one of the passengers commented, "You make it sound like you turned into the best version of yourself. Who you are, what makes you, you. Right?"

Dr. Ryons looked down and nodded. *Yes. Yes, I suppose so. What a nice way to put it.*

Then, after catching her breath, she'd finish.

I let go of the cloth. I know you must be wondering why. Now, I wonder too.

Here, I'd blush again, and then do a little curtsy, indicating that I had no more to say.

Curtsy? A curtsy! I haven't done that since I was a little girl. My mind is really on overload. A bell snapped Lissa out of her deep imaginings. Her racing thoughts halted. All five senses clicked back to normal.

The silent elevator doors split apart, displaying blank, neutral faces on strangers.

She stood still as if on pause.

A man's voice inquired, "Are you going down, Miss?"

"Oh, yes, I was, ah, am, I mean, that is. Sorry." Stepping in, she gladly turned her back to the eyes of the mini-audience. Like an unwanted companion, the smothering elevator silence added to her pumped-up uneasy state.

Dr. Ryons was first to step out at the street level. She briskly walked toward the exit.

Chapter 14

Leaving the climate-controlled building, Dr. Ryons stepped into New York's bitter cold winter. She murmured, *Not a Summer's eve!* The brightly lit front area of the Secretariat and circular driveway revealed the constant flow of snowflakes pushed on by a dark breeze. Below-freezing temperatures and a dose of wind made an unpleasant mix. She decided to take a cab back to her apartment instead of walking the two miles. She stood in the main doorway, zipping her coat even higher, and then passed two uninterested security guards.

Immediately, she heard harsh shouting and heckling voices from a group of protesters. This was nothing new for the U.N., being a popular visible location, like outside the White House or an embassy. These noise-makers positioned themselves on the sidewalk, the fringe zone—the nearest, so-called, public property. This meager string of people was in the half-light of the high sidewalk lampposts. Beneath them, on the cement pavement, their shadows followed every movement.

Islamists, again!

They operated in a loose, circling loop. Some held signs. One had a poorly done caricature of jolly Saint Nick, whom they labeled as "Satan Claus." *Oh boy! How clever.* Another one pictured a simplified painting of the United Nations Secretariat building. Across the top, red letters boldly read, "Worlds' Biggest PIG PEN."

Gosh! What a bunch of negative, critical people.

Four women wore the extreme, tent-style black burkas, leaving only a narrow slit for the eyes to peer at the world—in which they could not participate. Strangely, the five men wore modern street clothes.

Lissa thought, *Ladies, our world whirls on, with, or without you liking how it whirls!*

The women silently held their signs, only the men shouted. Some was in a Middle Eastern language, some in English. She heard the familiar "Allah Hu Akbar," meaning "God Is Great," as she recalled from the annual sensitivity classes, mandatory for all U.N. employees.

Though Dr. Ryons was a smart, educated woman, that intelligence never led her to follow international politics. Ironically, during these years spent employed at the core of the world's meeting place, she had immunized herself from its proceedings. The U.N.'s legal department rarely briefed her on the ramifications of Forensics findings. She preferred it that way. The lab ferreted out facts, sometimes with frightening international implications. In her career here, she joked to herself many times, *Politics? Down the hall and two flights up!*

Now, the angry strangers paraded in front of the huge building she knew as her home.

What do they want now? Don't they know it's Christmas time? Give it a rest. Due to the snow pack along the sidewalk, in order for a taxi to see her, she passed close to the group. An uncomfortable maneuver no matter who the protestors were, and whether day or night. She put on a practiced, neutral face of stone.

Ryons glanced at the group of nine protestors. Then she hurried toward a taxi. Passing close to one of the women, she read her sign. Like a high school homework project, several paper printouts taped together on cardboard, formed a quote. "Koran,

Sura 27:13, 14, When our miracles were done in their very sight, they said, 'This is obviously magic!' Though their souls knew them to be genuine … see what became of those evildoers!"

In Dr. Ryons' imagination, the word "magic" connected with the luminous napkin upstairs. She began thinking uncomfortable thoughts. *Is that strange cloth only a lost magician's prop? Or, maybe its phosphorescence is due to lousy laundry detergent.* These ideas stuck with a convincing clarity.

She unexpectedly locked eyes with the woman holding the sign—only for a brief moment, yet one in which time seemed to stretch and be still. A moment which Lissa would relive for the rest of her life.

As she walked farther, she felt something wasn't right. What was it? Besides the fact that the sign's message made no sense. A series of thoughts raced around her mind. *The woman who held the sign? The woman holding … the woman … but what … ? What about her? The eyes, those eyes. That's it—her eyes. The eyes … were all wrong. Hate-filled eyes. Not feminine at all. Plus those really thick eyebrows, a man's eyebrows!*

In the next few seconds, as the distance grew, she came to the waiting taxi. The processing ended with a scenario which fit. Anxious, she paused and looked back toward the protestors. Three screaming figures in burkas, threw aside their signs while running toward the U.N. entrance. No longer feeling the chill of winter, fear spiked her body with an overwhelming sweat.

But, it was already too late. The blast knocked her to the pavement.

- Part Three -

Chapter 15

Before the distraction and pressure of the Christmas and New Year's holidays, plus the temporary closing of the U.N. after the attack, the Linguistics team discovered little about the napkin. That is, until they stopped looking at contemporary languages and started looking backward. They sent photographs of the inscription writing style to a third party, to target experts in ancient languages in the U.S. and abroad. This unknown cousin resembled variants of ancient Sumerian, Egyptian and Hebrew.

Dr. Ryons knew nothing of the Linguistics' department efforts. Waiting for the results of the farmed-out cloth seemed endless to her. What little momentum the project gained since her return, turned green, slowing down because Saint Patrick's Day gaiety had struck. Extra beer nights at local pubs after work, cookies with green sprinkles and the downtown parade did their business zapping concentration. Even the gift shop sent Dr. Ryons a big flower, with spray painted lime green petals and glitter; and to top it off, clover nestled around the stem. She rolled her eyes in frustration. While making the phone call to return the order, and curtly request a plain non-green flower—she noticed a one-half inch tall leprechaun glued to the edge of a petal, seated and waving to all the world. No. Not for her. Instead, she avoided heading into a day of cutesy compliments and inquiries of possible Irish lineage which would've drawn blank stares from the doctor.

Back to the napkin specimen. Tired of waiting, Dr. Ryons went to plan B. She approached the U.N.'s graphic design department to find out what stirred in artists' imaginations when viewing the carefully drawn, peculiar letters and diagrams. The artsy crew took an interest in this side project since it meant a break from 'work as usual.' Common adverts, brochures and posters only stimulated certain parts of the creative brain—a needy scientist presenting her own Rorschach test shook things up. When, after several days, they failed to define or interpret the examples in any useful way, Dr. Ryons' annoyance went up a notch. *Nothing helpful from them, only empty ideas, useless concepts and educated burps! Honestly, did they even graduate from high school? I bet they get together after work, smoke cannabis, play acoustic guitars with patchouli incense plugging up their partially-working brains.*

Next, with Mr. Griffin's approval, she sent out photographs of the napkin's two sides—designated Side One and Side two—to the four out-sourced universities. What came back a few weeks later convinced her that the U.N. graphics employees must have graduated from those same four universities. *I get queasy just thinking that those people get a respectable weekly paycheck.*

Well into April, Dr. Ryons lost her patience. One day, she decided to harness the progressive idea to simply go public with the indecipherable writings and peculiar diagrams. An email from Donald Griffin gave her the approval to pursue her idea. She berated herself for not having done this sooner. Her fellow lab workers took the brunt of that well-brewed anger. If only Lissa's eyes could read their fretful faces. Each wished they'd stayed home from work that day or could find a quick reason to leave early.

Her doctor removed the annoying arm sling and brace and refilled her prescription of pain pills. Lingering brain trauma birthed more than one wild card in an otherwise normal deck. Discussing her obsession *Was it obsession?* made her consider seeing an on-staff psychologist. But, she shook her head with an ache—followed by a shooting pain down her neck. *No.*

Finally she strove for the next strategy. She thought, *After an unbelievable amount of protocol and kissing ass, clearance comes through for extra funding to exhibit the mystery on the gallery walls of the U.N. lobbies. Yeah, well, what the hell, let's put some people to work and spend the world's money!* The look on her face had a scary twist to it. Only the crew worker, Marge, viewed this grimace and she fumbled whatever was in her hands.

With Lar's assistance, Dr. Ryons counted 14 distinct sections from the two sides. She commissioned the U.N. Graphics department to refine the 14 in Photoshop and enlarged into digital prints 40 inches square. From her U.N. purse she hired a staff interior designer to purchase contemporary frames and to place the pictures behind glass. In all, there were 3 copies of each design for 3 concurrent displays located in the lobbies of the Conference and Visitor's Center, the General Assembly Building and the Secretariat Tower.

The 42 pictures ate little into the U.N.'s overall budget. The Office of the Comptroller agreed to allow the expenditures on two conditions. First, the exhibit would last three weeks and not one day more. Second, after the exhibit, the individual pieces would be auctioned off online or sold directly to any inquirers to recoup the monies spent on "her" project. A third unspoken, but implied condition was for the fidgety, pushy scientist to not set foot in their office for a goodly length of time after the installation of the shows.

The current artistic exhibition portraying the Children's Plight in Thailand simply disappeared one day. On the next appeared consecutively numbered images of Napkin Doodle Art. Dr. Ryons was proud of herself. She visited the displays as soon as the contractors finished installing the pieces. She crossed her arms and let loose a smirk and lengthy sarcastic smile, saying out loud to no one, "Doodle Art, yeah right!"

She didn't know that at midnight, members of the *shadows* visited each of the 42 framed pictures. Using ladders, costly high-tech devices with specialized micro tools and orders from one Donald Griffin, teams accomplished a dark task.

Ryons recycled her hopes to spread the baffling language and detailed diagrams even farther and wider—whatever it took. She loved a challenge and this item—a napkin—though not recognized, had hooked her heart much more than it did her prideful, analytical intellect. The mysterious cloth, with its deliberate designs and messages, dared her, calling her to "figure me out!" That one touch, four months ago, caused an infection which would prove to have no cure. The symptoms fused parts of her heart together, long forgotten and unwanted ones but necessary for life—not in perceptible ways, not yet. What drove her went beyond her weekly paycheck. The personal overtime was the right use of time.

The next morning Ryons entered the lobby to see her endeavor. She murmured, "Get to work guys. Grab some attention and answers for me." She briefly visited the other two lobby exhibits and smiled. Ryons hoped her bored hours of hospital time would pay off with yet another idea. To accelerate results at the three exhibits, she requested, and was granted, by Mr. Donald Griffin, that the U.N. station "informed or knowledgeable" security guards. This request also included for two hours a day, certain low-rung U.N. employees, such as interns, mail room sorters, and coffee chasers, rotating as undercover admirers. Each dummy viewer volunteered to be wired with enhanced listening devices to overhear conversations that might provide clues. Any notable intel was funneled upstairs. These listening devices fell into Dr. Ryons' hands after discussing the idea with Don Griffin...who asked no questions and placed no hurdles. *Thank God for that!*

Aside from this varied intricate web work of her imagination, and unknown to Lissa, the *shadows* rigged each frame with micro cameras and microphones. Of course, conventional surveillance ceiling cameras covered the lobbies 24/7. Combined, these made the three exhibits the most technologically monitored graphics exhibit in U.S. history.

Chapter 16

Dr. Ryons took the elevator to the U.N.'s Website Design department to set in motion her next and last idea birthed on the hospital bed. The Internet was the largest and last step. She originally hoped that it wouldn't be necessary to go this far and the fabric mystery solved weeks ago. *I'm not getting any younger!*

Her appointment with one of the webmasters and his assistants proved upbeat with high expectations. She handed the webmaster a flash drive and briefed the staff on the short history of the cloth. He copied the data, which also included files outlining the meager entirety of the napkin including Web-ready graphics. Dr. Ryons proceeded with her PowerPoint presentation, which the graphics department supplied, or rather, she forced them to create. After her narration ended, no hands went up for questions.

After that, she said, "I want you to throw a big fishing net w-a-y out there and catch fish with sharp brains! You figure out what bait to use."

The man saw the look on the doctor's face, which read, *There's nothing to ask, just provide me the damn results!*

He also recalled the story of Doctor Ryons and the Christmas bombing. Besides other injuries, she took quite a blow on the head, a traumatic experience and then lost considerable time in the hospital recuperating. This made him wonder if a jarred part of her brain didn't get plugged back in correctly.

So, without her knowing it, he suppressed voicing the trendy expression, *W-h-a-t-e-v-e-r!?!* Instead, he gave her an intelligent smile which passed on the impression that he "got it." Behind that "look" resided a false depth of understanding, coupled with meager interest, which was one of his favorite faces. This expression got him through a lot of very boring U.N. staff meetings—besides helping to keep his job secure.

First, Ryons requested the IT people work with the bohemian gang in graphics to create a stand alone, viral, infomercial. Hopefully, this would draw people to the U.N.'s website. The new web pages for the unusual U.N. exhibitions needed a cool look to get online looky-lous to settle down and focus. IT chose these Tag Words: mysterious, mind bending, enigma, esoteric, mischief, colorful, intelligent, matchless, draws-you-in, strange art, puzzle, weird, lost and found, doodle and napkin.

Unleashed originality among the web designers brought smiles, knowing their daily tedium could take a quirky turn of direction. They joked about it as the "Napkin Extravaganza Project" or "Napkin-palooza" and "Burning Man's Napkin." A running jest involved having the napkin's designs enlarged for a custom hot air balloon. Imaginative advertising pop-ups interrupted visitors. These had a special, but temporary dispensation on certain pages of the official United Nations' website, which directed the curious to the napkin sister-site.

Second, the U.N.'s main website's homepage provided a link to a dazzling site with doodle-art games, puzzles, gimmicks and a "Contact Us" link. The employees enjoyed showing off their skills using the new features of the latest software programs and apps. Thanks to an Adobe plug-in, one graphic artist devised an activity in which the 14 diagrams actually looked like 3-D puzzle pieces. These puzzles had increasing levels of difficulty with corresponding point values. Gamers could compete against the clock or against other online players.

IT suggested to Dr. Ryons a napkin Twitter account. But, she couldn't grasp the point and wanted to veto the idea, but finally let out a "W-h-a-t-e-v-e-r." *Only 140 characters! What is this, the Stone Age of technology beating a weansy-sized drum?* A Facebook page and a YouTube channel played close-ups of the diagrams and written language. Exotic New Age music looped in the background. This lush geek paradise had a good chance of the project turning a challenging invisible corner.

One of the other online gimmicks was a Guess-What-I-Am? What-do-you-see? forum. Under the United Nations logo, these online brainteaser projects were sent to art schools and art department inboxes nationwide. Having come from the U. N., this educational curiosity dutifully caught teachers and administrators attention.

Dr. Ryons' number three idea? Give stuff away to create incentive. Top ranked thinkers could win tickets to location specific cultural events—even rock or symphony concerts. Providing the opportunity to earn decent rewards for participation was a must for Ryons. *We'll sucker 'em in!* Municipalities with museums or art galleries gladly donated a small amount of tickets for the presages United Nations efforts.

Within days, inquiries about the unique graphics trickled in. The fishing lines in the ever-flowing, deep cyber waters experienced tugging from around the globe. The webmaster was satisfied, Ryons smiled with anticipation, and a growing number of U.N. workers in different departments sensed accomplishment in the near future.

The U.N. housed two especially interested parties. Only one knew why they were so interested. Lissa thought, *Maybe my job or career has lost its challenge? This whole thing is a little overboard and nutty.* She tried to rationalize the extra expense and manpower spent on a curiosity which might end with no useful data. *Not good for my resume!*

But the other party protected its own motives, and had no budget worries. They eyed the project with their own private questions and desired answers. Unbeknownst to Ryons this camp kept opening the otherwise locked doors she continually passed through. For all her passion and persistence, on her own, Dr. Lissa Ryons simply did not have that kind of pull at the U.N.

Yet, the big blanks of why she was doing all of this, remained to be filled in. Would it all be worth it when the answers arrived? While in her office, occasional streaks of dizziness and giddiness swept through Ryons. Though sitting, she gripped the edge of her desk. After this involuntary rush, worry seemed to grow from the floor up surrounding her. She pulled open a desk drawer and held an orange bottle of medication. She stared. *Sane brain pills. Just maybe.*

Chapter 17

The first FedEx package arrived from University Number One. For them it was just another anonymous research project. As long as the university got its check and their laboratory got its cut, all were smiles.

The report stated the various dating methods utilized on the triangular shaped sample of cloth. The findings caused Lissa to shake her head and file the hard copy paperwork away for now. *One down, three to go.*

Even if the U.N. included paperwork explaining what little they knew about the cloth samples, such information would have barely filled a single page.

Her forensics lab worked on other projects, but this one oddity whirled in the space that took up the back of the boss' mind, much like a computer program running unnoticed in the background.

The tests did not find fingerprints or DNA evidence, but Dr. Ryons had known that. She corrected herself, *I had a pretty good guess it would be so.*

In preparing her report for the U.N. Linguistics department, she sifted through the findings. One comment stood out: "The ink used by the originator of the document is truly an anomaly, no traces of animal, plant, vegetable, mineral or man-made synthetics. Substance unknown." She thought, *What? The researchers have never come across any chemical compound like it before? Geez!*

She continued reading, "Recommendations: collect ink and dye samples used for archival writings, artwork and decorative objects from modern day remote villages and retrieve artifacts from ancient tribes. Museums and private collections essential."

This professional advice of "collecting and retrieving" struck her as laughable.

Pained with sharp annoyance, she scrunched up her face and said in a mocking tone to no one in particular, "Great idea! I'll just take a sabbatical for…oh, ten or more years. I'll travel this *sooo* safe world of ours, collecting ink samples for the good ol' U.N." She paused. "For a napkin!" Frustrated, head down, eyes shut, angst rippled through her body. Through her tight jaw, out came, "Damn, I'm mad and I want results now! A month ago, a week ago! Now!"

In a nervous spasm, she awkwardly jutted her elbows, as knees and shoulders wriggled. *What was that? Something leftover from my brain injury or what? Weird.* She looked around the lab thankfully no one had seen the twitching.

Dr. Ryons plunked down at her computer to conjure up a straight line to the goal of a solid, reasonable solution. That is, she wanted to think, but her mystified mind repeatedly blanked out. Again, she couldn't help wondering if the concussion's effects left areas of her brain still needing servicing. But she didn't want one more minute of medical attention, or worse, mental inspection. *I'll just ride this out and keep track of any involuntary physical behavior while under stress—or not.*

Impulsively, she picked up the phone to call somebody who could take this napkin investigation to another level—a level that provided answers. While holding the phone pondering whom to call, her eyes stared at nothing. That is, until a recorded voice broke the void in her mind, "If you would like to make a call please hang-up and try again…If you woo…." She slammed it down in the receiver.

There was no one to call, not yet. Closing her eyes, she thought, *This is one heck of a wild goose chase and all I've got are feathers... I guess I'll wait for more goose feathers to arrive.*

Other "feathers" arrived within a week and she gratefully read the reports. "All four universities are playing the dating game, but what game am I playing? Feather chaser? Yes. Goose getter? No."

Dr. Ryons' exhaustion merged with sly amusement, stirring her increasing annoyance. *Maybe I'll use a glue gun and stick all of these feathers together. Yeah that's it. I'd have that goose right here, hollow though it would be... and that's alright, really!* Then she slumped, and repeatedly flicked a thumb nail between her teeth. This made a click sound every few seconds. *Great! I'm chewing my nails again... haven't done that one for a few years. I'm getting a headache just thinking about getting a headache.*

Chapter 18

The cloth's glow affected Dr. Ryons; those pleasant, desirable feelings when she had touched the fabric. Ryons also feared losing physical control over the specimen. Of the Forensics departments' variety of routine investigations, her over the top fascination seemed to rise out of nowhere to her co-workers.

Shortly after her return from the hospital, she added another secret to her private after hours routine. She'd lock the entry door; turn off the lights, except a small one to see by. In the darkness, during those quiet times, she opened the drawer where the napkin lie. Taking out the metal specimen tray and leaning against a counter, she simply stared at the corner-less, glowing square. A cigarette? That would have completed the ritual. But she didn't and couldn't. In her private evening "research," she never arrived at why it glowed … it just did. Did the material have an unidentifiable chemical reaction which affected a person's psyche, creating feelings of goodness and peace? By touching the material or standing close, did it cause the release of euphoric chemicals in the brain, like a narcotic substance does? She wondered over and over again. But, she really didn't want to know the truth. Her feminine heart yearned not to ruin her private mystery.

She recalled the first day when the sample arrived in the lab. "Each person inhaled, but each nasal cavity identified a different scent or odor—all were pleasant fragrances, nothing foul—almost selective. Perhaps the cloth emits a chemical which releases chemicals from our olfactory nerves connecting to where pleasant memories reside? Once in the nostrils it activates a random memory. But the blind studies lacked any detection using the faculty of smell by machine or man."

Ryons bent her neck forward, "I still smell chamomile, that's all."

She didn't see the yellow-bluish luminosity as eerie. While staring at it, whatever her rough feelings leftover from that workday always changed, lessening, so a pleasant composure prevailed. She'd think, *Dr. Ryons, you need your evening dose of Napkin-eze.*

Then and again, while viewing, emotions overcame her, whose winding trails disappeared in a mist. Lissa would cry. She had no specific subject or memories stirring which changed her into a weeping woman. The tears cleansed her. She didn't want to cry. Yet, when the crying started, Lissa didn't try to block it or veer from her personal fountain and shut it down. She counted the drops as dear, strange, but dear. Though nameless and unidentifiable, each was a friend filling a pool in which one day she might see a true reflection of herself.

Before leaving for home, Dr. Ryons always put the strange cargo back into its drawer. She never handled the object with her fingers, only sterile tongs, especially if she wanted to turn it over. She didn't want to touch it and feel that...*was it magic? Nooo, not again! Wherever this connection comes from ... is certainly foreign.* If she were to hold it, she feared wanting to keep it as her own possession; but it belonged to the United Nations. The line she didn't want to cross was holding it close to her chest, or against her face. It seemed the cloth would become like a precious handkerchief or gift of delicate lace. Self-control mixed with professionalism always prevailed. *Perhaps I could buy it off the U.N. and take it home, nah ... ?*

She admired, yet kept a queer distance from this calming, wordless, stranger. She valued the good energy, even though she had felt it only once at full strength. Touching the cloth would be too enticing and she felt unsure of where that might take her. *Full strength? Is there even more narcotic effect? I did touch one corner for... well, how long was that? Two seconds...two minutes...or twenty!* In her teen years, on a couple of forgettable dates, she became intoxicated with alcohol. *Beer and wine don't mix well!* Once, just to fit in, she tried marijuana, but all that happened to her, besides hunger, were feelings of paranoia.

The force propelling Lissa came from behind and before her. Caught in the middle? She knew this late night sensation too well. She never considered quitting the hunt for the napkin's origins. To say "No!" merely passed through her mind like a thin, drifting vapor.

*   *   *

In her meager preliminary report to Don Griffin, and the duplicate report forwarded to the U.N. Secretary General, Dr. Ryons did not note the luminosity or her emotional experience. She felt no guilt about excluding the phenomenon, rationalizing, *Those reports just end up in the huge archival database read by no one.* The few lab visitors, via Mr. Donald Griffin, who came to inspect the object, weren't informed about the luminescence either. She kept this fact guarded. "Please don't touch the fabric. The specimen is still under research." Lissa feared herself jumping between a visitor and the napkin if they reached out a hand. *Please, no. Don't do that.*

On some days when work slowed up or during break time, Dr. Ryons openly studied the cloth. *It's better than reading the newspaper, a magazine or stupid stuff on the Internet.* She kept her distance, not wanting to get emotional.

The crew saw their boss' napkin meditation as a quirky change due to continuing recovery of brain trauma. This behavior seemed harmless and therapeutic for their typically high-strung, impersonal boss. Why intrude? An unseen observer might think she was covering something up—in the same way she would keep concealed an injury to a private and clothed part of her body.

But, in fact, Dr. Ryons intended telling the crew about the paranormal news on her first day back at work. But, she never did. She left this fact out though she didn't know or understand what motivated her unprofessional secrecy. She sometimes wondered why and what stopped her telling anyone about the wonderful occurrence on the night of the bombing—but had no conclusions. A shadowy congealing of emotions and half-thoughts simmered like a miniature treadmill in the inner closet of her mind. And mixed with that, resided a degree of fault. Lissa knew she was incapable of properly expressing the oddity to her coworkers. That is, unless after telling them, they volunteered to touch the specimen in the dark and see if what happened to her, happened to them also.

But, no one knew, but her.

Ryons told herself on many trips in the elevator, *One morning, as soon as I walk in the door, I'll act surprised about how I stumbled on the luminous properties and accidentally touched it the night before. Then it will all be okay and over with.*

But other, more pressing duties came and went through the department. During one particular week, a top-priority project from the higher-ups absorbed most of their days. The possibility of a dirty bomb factory (in an undisclosed location), had increased significantly. Haz-mat samples and other potential evidence arrived at the lab under U.N. guard. Having stationed, armed, uniformed men with blue berets in the lab made the crew uneasy. No one joked about anything. A rumor spread that if the lab-results were what everybody hoped they wouldn't be, a U.N. sanctioned air strike would result. That bit of information slipped out from one of the military who hadn't been properly briefed on lab protocol. This created an added air of tension to the stress level.

When work had settled back down one day, during break-time, Dr. Ryons once again pondered the cloth on its tray—a little too dreamily for her coworkers comfort. They all gave their boss an extra dose of independence since her return. Her head injury might have made her less focused and more distractible than before. No one knew what medications she might be taking or how many.

Lars quietly came and stood next to her.

Noting her ritual enchantment with the napkin, he broke in by greeting her, "How's our Doctor today?" Stroking his beard, he nodded a little. After the silence of a minute or so and no reply, he added, "It's a unique dining table accessory. Gives one a peaceful, serene feeling, doesn't it?"

Blood raced to her face. Reddening cheeks possessed the color of embarrassment. Dumbfounded; her jaw dropped, paused, and then slowly closed. Involuntarily, she bristled as disappointment pulsed through her body with the unpleasant warmth. Her times of viewing and secret ones in the evening were…were they over? *All this time at work have I looked like a fool staring at a weird dinner napkin?*

To Dr. Ryons, it sounded as if he spoke in a common manner, such as holding a plate of donuts, asking her if she wanted glazed or plain. Sizzling, she turned to look up into Lars' eyes. She peered intently, inflamed with quizzical earnestness. Trying to restrain herself, in a tight voice she asked, "What did you say? What, what do you mean Lars?"

He responded, "Oh, you know, when all the lights are dimmed and it…sits there and glows in its innocent way…giving off luminescence…just enough to let you know it's there and not normal, not really something like us. Not from around here, you might say."

She stiffened, mentally repeating Lars's observation, '*Not one of us?*' *God, he said that as if it has having self-awareness or a personality. How bizarre!*

Lars continued, "We've all taken turns chewing on different ideas. We've been wondering what the boss conjured up in her noodle about our friend here?"

Her head dropped. Without knowing her actions, Ryons reached up to the flower in her button hole (a yellow pansy) and crumpled it. Lars noticed the extra release of fragrance wrought by its demise. The damaged flower fell.

She wondered, *When did the lab techs sneak in their viewing without my being aware? Why wasn't I professional? Why didn't I share my discovery with them? Why didn't they, being employees, fill me in? Now, I need to come up with a plausible excuse. When it comes down to it, being their boss doesn't exempt me from cooperation. It's what I expect from them. Perhaps they did it while I was at my many unpleasant occupational therapy appointments?*

Dr. Ryons let her guard down just enough in hopes to get some answers from Lars. She tried to act like she was no dummy about the goings on in her lab and to speak without a hint of surprise. Making her best guess, she said, "So…lunch hour in the lab has become a collective Deep Thought time around here?" referring to, author Douglas Adams' "Deep Thought" character from *Hitchhiker's Guide to the Galaxy*. Ryons' sly remark slammed at their deep thoughts and reckonings, *Done without my permission or supervision.*

Lars caught the glib edge in her voice, bolstering the slight sneer on her face—and he'd seen the movie, too. He surmised that his boss thought she, and only she, knew that the napkin was special. He literally saw her out-of-the-ordinary isolated secret, angrily dissolve. The heel of one of her shoes began repeatedly banging on the cabinet behind her. Lars looked down to investigate, then tilted his head to see right into her face. Startled, he perceived something like a violation of her supposed sovereignty as mistress of the United Nations Forensics Laboratories.

She steamed with annoyance; all the techs below her, had moseyed into her most private of realms. But there really wasn't a "realm," just employees in white lab coats, meandering under bright fluorescent lights, who daily trod on hard linoleum floors while monotonously sipping coffee.

Lars let her hissy comment dissipate into nothingness. Then he did some quick thinking and attempted a jest about the item. "Doctor, maybe the Shroud of Turin was finally sent out to be laundered. After all those centuries of being dingy and … it shrank? After that it was neatly folded and being unrecognizable; someone innocently doodled on it at the Vatican Cleaners … and it ended up here by accident!" He sped up for comic emphasis. "So, what do you think?" He looked at her with a meant-to-amuse, pasted on, silly grin.

This ploy didn't get any validation from her.

He heard her reply stated firmly and without a strand of humor.

"The 'Shroud' doesn't glow!" Stomping her foot, Lissa turned to go sulk in her office. With clenched fists, Lissa let out a frenzied screech no one heard. "Damn, damn...damn! I want to know now!" She reached up to fidget with her flower and looked down only feeling her empty button hole. Her face scrunched in curiosity wondering where the flower had gone to.

She wanted the truth about why that thing glowed, where it came from, who the hell wrote the esoteric language and diagrams, why was it in her lab and lastly—in her head.

Chapter 19

Lissa Ryons did not hate men, but she clutched bitterness about the mis-use by men in her past. She kept these memories hidden; no counseling sessions, self-help books or confidential conversations over coffee with a girlfriend. She kept "research" for laboratory work only. Her meager social life entirely drifted away when she relocated to New York. Yes, her heart needed to become a soft landing pad for a good man to land on, to bless, and to love. Her busy, wound-up, lifeless self needed someone to love her into sweet silence. But the heart lived with sores and existed indefinitely closed to men-hood. *Men-ace,* she thought.

Lars was the closest, warmest man in her life. To her, he was like having a distant brother who occasionally came by for a brief visit and a snack.

One morning while pinning on a burgundy zinnia, she noticed an aphid on a petal. This had not happened before. The tiny intruder on the perfect bloom summed up her attitude of people desiring to commune and bond with her. She went through a process of deciding what to do to the bug: shake the flower, flick a fingernail on the petal, squeeze the hobo between two fingertips or, using a scissor, trim off the petal over a waste can. She chose to do what she did with people—cut off the life raft whose lone occupant was an unwanted participant. After a surgical snip, the yellow petal fluttered spiraling into the trash. She grabbed the can and took it to a containment unit with a lid, emptied it and returned to her office.

Is Lars like an aphid I've allow in my life? I know he means me no harm. Plus, he's married n' all.

Lissa returned to her keyboard, typed, and sent a spicy complaint. At the U.N. floral gift shop, the email read by the attendant, caused her to blink, press her face closer to the screen to make sure she really read what she had. A finger waved for her boss to come over, who said, "Forensics. Dr. Ryons, ohh, yes, hmm. Never met her, and I'm not looking forward to, if that day ever comes. It only takes one weensy bug to really bug that woman."

The clerk used her still poised finger and drilled it into her bosses' side making her wiggle. The clerk stated, "Takes one to know one. Does it dear? Hah!"

* * *

The following day, after the disclosure of the napkin, Lars couldn't hold back his curiosity about something which took place after the bombing. That mysterious phrase the nurse said Dr. Ryons repeated in I.C.U., while under medication. His boss appeared in a good mood. He hesitantly ventured to her office, tapped on the door, went in, then closed it.

"Oh, please leave it open Lars, I could use the air, she said."

Lars noticed a pink rose pinned to her lab coat. "Beautiful flower Doctor, wonderful fragrance."

She gazed up at him with a quizzical, lost look. He might as well have notified her that the sun rose again that day.

He sucked in his lips at her peculiar response and blank eyes. "Doctor, I'd like to ask you something that might be personally, ahh...disturbing. May I?"

She nodded an apprehensive *Go ahead.*

"At the hospital, one of the nurses said you repeatedly mumbled a peculiar phrase—'stage car go.' I'm curious, what does that mean—if anything? Apparently you said these words with some importance." He stood leaning against the door frame waiting.

"Huh? I don't know…" She stopped and did some mental cross referencing. "Lars…I think that was from the meds," she explained with a slight upturn of a smile.

Dr. Ryons looked at Lars and read that he felt a little stupid for asking. His face clearly showed, *Okay, nothing but a slur of words dreamed up by a dripping mixture of pain killers and sedatives.*

But a further explanation surprised him.

In an amused tone she volunteered, "Yes, I might have said something sounding like that, but I meant 'strange cargo'—two words. Not "stage", but strange; "cargo," like a package on a ship. *Strange Cargo* is a movie, that my hus…ah, that I saw many years ago."

While revising her explanation, she shifted her eyes away from Lars. During her three years at the U.N. she had never shared anything about her failed marriage or her ex-husband. Her three children, though not in the same hands-off category, rarely came up in conversation.

Lars' caught her subtle body language.

She continued, "It's a great old black and white film from the 1940s staring Clark Gable and Joan Crawford. I remember it well. The story featured a bizarre but wonderful character named Cambreau. He appears out of nowhere on this Devil's Island, jungle penal colony. He wasn't a convict or even a criminal, but he dressed like the prisoners. Actually, none of the prisoners had ever seen him before. So, they assumed he was the newest inmate.

"Shortly after his arrival, he joined a dozen men on a well-planned prison breakout. In the midst of this variety of criminals, Cambreau begins to influence each man. He draws out something good which still resided in them, I guess…deep in their personalities … or souls, some would call it. He knew how to restore honor in each one—usually, just before they died during the adventurous ill-fated escape attempt.

"It was 'strange,'" Lissa caught herself and chuckled, realizing the coincidence of the medically induced word confusion. "Strange, indeed. Cambreau knew things about each person, things about their heart, what made them who they were. Mildly supernatural perhaps, but not silly or superstitious, not over-the-top like a lot of today's movies."

She grinned, "They wanted him to be by their side, be their friendly protector, confidante. He was like the unexpected but desired person in your life. He—whoever he was, well … he purposely chose to be their escort and then attempted to guide whoever would listen. Along the way, one prisoner after another dies. Each time Cambreau attempts to locate their heart. I suppose, being a servant of goodness or whatever, to show the way to rest from their long labors of wrong doing; the weariness of their warped lives, sin is how some blame it.

"In the escape, the mismatched gang manages to get a boat for their voyage to the mainland. This single man, who had no apparent reason to be counted as a criminal, influenced these ruffians, this desperate crew. A 'strange cargo' joined the boat's passengers."

This got Lars' full attention. He said, "Sounds like a movie I'd enjoy watching with Adelina. I'll look it up on Netflix when I get home." The big man tilted his head and hoped for more information. "What happened to this mysterious, imitation convict? Also, what's the connection?"

"Cambreau? At the end, you almost expect him to sprout wings and fly away. But he just turns and walks off, and the movie ends. Oh! Only two changed or improved convicts survived." She thoughtfully considered the mysterious napkin and how to correctly express her personal thread of ideas, yet remain professional. *Why did that old movie come out of the depths of my memory so many years later?*

Standing unnoticed in the open doorway, the lab tech, Marge, had quietly joined them. She volunteered, "The luminous, doodled-up napkin is kind of like the U.N.'s strange cargo, right Doctor Ryons? This all started in our lost and found." She spoke innocently, a mild tone of sincerity mixed with confidence.

Neither Lissa nor Lars appeared intruded upon by the listener. He stroked his beard in new thoughts. Ryons gave an affirming nod, simply adding, "And if so, to what end?"

Chapter 20

After work, Lars and Adelina met at the U.N.'s east side temporary entrance. Earlier in the day the couple had made plans to have dinner out. Now they walked to the subway and then strolled to their favorite Thai restaurant, Canoey Louie's. Adelina recognized the withdrawn mood of her husband. Should she roll her eyes or show compassion? Instead she chose to get out her phone to text and tend to emails. In their marriage she'd been here, and done that before. Lars, pre-occupied, he wouldn't say a word. Some days his dark moods just took longer to wear off than others.

After ten minutes she decided to do her marital duty. "Hun, what's on your mind? You haven't said a word. Trouble at the lab, hmm?" She heard a grunt in response.

They arrived at Louie's, where miniature hand-carved Thai and Asian style canoes served as plates. On the customer's birthday, Louie's serves ice cream on a special boat with tiny Thai flags. When the couple entered, their faces brightened in the strong spicy atmosphere. Green bamboo stalks and leaves lined the walls and mats of narrow dried bamboo lined the ceiling. Candles in colorful glass containers lit every table. Southeast Asian music played over the loudspeakers. They reached their table, and for a moment Lars focused on the colorful blooming silk flowers around the restaurant. When seated at a booth, facing each other, his isolation crumbled.

Lars waved off their waiter's offer of menus. Instead, he cheerfully instructed, "Two number twenty-threes; three stars. Two Thai ice teas before the food arrives please." Dating a Latina had caused Lars to expand his spice tolerance. Adelina tolerated his weakness and refrained from five stars. A women's magazine article on "cultural differences versus marriage companionship" recommended such "livable balances."

The waiter nodded. "As always, sir." People easily remembered the friendly, big Norwegian.

Lars added, "Oh, tonight I'm really hungry. Bring the Coconut Prawns appetizer; one star."

He enjoyed Adelina's brown skin, dark eyes and long black hair styled today with large curls in a wonderful way.

In the dim atmosphere the two held hands across the table. Each looked into the other's eyes. Adelina spoke first, which wasn't unusual in their marriage. "Hun, you've been under stress at the lab. Too much tension for too long, my love. What can you tell me?"

Lars' mouth opened and then closed. He stared down at their clasped hands. While nodding in agreement he said, "Yes."

"Hun, what can you tell me? What can I do for you?"

The big man hadn't envisioned this dialogue, and quick answers evaded him. The iced teas arrived. He sipped while searching for the core of his stress, just the right answers. U.N. security protocols shadowed the information to draw from. His wife knew that limitations restricted such conversation. Lars eyed the ceiling as his lower jaw strained to one side. After a deep breath he started. "Adelina, at the time near The Tragedy, a specimen came into the lab. Simply put, since then Dr. Ryons hasn't been right in the head. It's tough to sort out her head injuries and meds…and… these other behaviors. She's drawn to this object…mesmerized. She pulls it out of the specimen drawers, leaves it on the metal tray and stares. Lunch time, after work and sometimes in the morning before the crew shows up, yet she never touches it." His large hands spread open.

His wife let her drink wait and listened attentively. "Have you discussed this with anyone else in the lab crew?" He shook his head. "Is Ryons making," she paused, apparently seraching for the correct word, "foolish, yes, foolish decisions or showing incompetency that's a danger to you or anyone?" He shook again. She hesitated, then stated, "Lars, have you considered going over her head with this?"

He leaned to one side of the booth, his eyes squinted. "Why do you have to be so clinical, so damn impersonal?" His angry face settled into a stone.

The canoe with four prawns and sauce arrived. Adelina nibbled on one of the prawns. Lars shoved one in his mouth after the other, barely chewing.

Adelina's head lowered a notch, her lips set to retaliate. A grunt came before she spoke. "Why? We've been through this before. I'm a secretary where personal input and interaction can get you into trouble. There's a playbook of do's and don't's. Y' know, some days I feel like a machine or computer website. I do what I'm told— nothing more. I'm not paid to act friendly, only to perform. My personality is not required, efficiency is. On an average day I speak with 65 people, 60 who usually are strangers. Some speak Spanish, but most have foreign strong accents or speak little English. Each expects too much from me. Okay? So, my dear husband, whom I love, I ask why the stress? What worries you?" She made an artificial smile, took a long sip of her tea and stared him down.

As Lars ignored his wife's quick fury. He muttered, "Why?" He picked up his white cloth napkin from his lap and raised it high and square for his wife to see.

She squinted in perplexed curiosity. "What the heck is this? Are you going to do a trick with that to make my anger go away, dear? Or, are you surrendering to your sulking mood?"

"Honey, let's reset. I apologize, please forgive. Honest." He let that sink in for effect. "My boss is infatuated with a napkin, just like this one."

Extending one hand, Adelina stopped him. "Are you making up a story?" The waiter passed by and she caught his attention. "Yes. Please switch my Number 23 to five stars."

Lars wilted and lowered the napkin. "The napkin is special."

"Looks like every napkin in this place!"

Lars lowered his head and took a deep breath. "Hun, I'm not at liberty to fully answer the 'why' of your original question. Dr. Ryons has gone…."

"Kooky!"

"No, cuckoo is more like it. She's received funding from upstairs to research this—that napkin. Understand, dear, on both sides of the white fabric are amazing diagrams and a written language no one can decipher. That's all I can say about the specimen. The point is, I'm very concerned about my boss. This obsession of hers has claws and she's reaching out every way imaginable. Upstairs is supportive and Dr. Ryons just keeps going."

Her eyes softened and in a sincere tone she said, "I'll ask my mother to light a candle at church for your boss. Okay?"

Their meal arrived. Five boats held Thai cuisine. As always, the waiter took a step back remaining to see if the guests desired anything else.

Adelina spoke up, "Bring my husband a beer, a tall one. He needs it!"

- Part Four -

Chapter 21

Dr. Ryons functioned in a strained relationship with the suited, snooping *shadows*. She suspected something more sophisticated going on in her lab than the tiny ceiling-mounted surveillance camera in the examination room. She imagined that in all 39 floors of the U.N. Secretariat Tower, discreet video and listening devices lived in every toilet stall and water cooler station. *Not really such bad locations for a place like this!* Private and hushed brief cell phone calls made in restrooms happened constantly, plus one-on-one personal conversations at photocopiers and water coolers. *Probably got some spying going on there too.*

Two years ago she stopped rapping on the walls of her laboratory, expecting to hear a knock-knock coming back. She no longer ran her fingers along the backs of tall file cabinets looking for a secret latch, suspecting it would swing out revealing an opening to a spiral stairway. Like passageways in a medieval castle, she imagined the *shadows* using them for secret comings and goings in the important U.N. offices.

Don Griffin of *shadow central* emailed Dr. Ryons. He wanted to have a meeting concerning the progress her department and his linguistics team had come up with. The meeting would be on the following Tuesday at 10 a.m. in a small conference room of his choosing.

"Always their choosing," Lissa half-muttered.

Dr. Ryons came armed with her U.N. issued laptop, an optimistic view and an uncomfortable streak of curiosity. Early in her employment, Lissa first eyed Don Griffin when passing him in a hallway. She took in his out-of-joint looks with amusement, wondering at what age he'd stopped wearing broken eyeglasses, taped together at the bridge of the nose. She heard a fart by him and assumed such tailwind typical daily hallway exhaust.

She entered a cheerless conference room. No paintings or pictures broke the monotony of the light gray putty-colored walls. And whatever anybody's mood, the carpeting would pull it down to the foot worn floor and keep it there. Six dark gray, folding metal chairs surrounded a plain metal table with fake wood grain veneer. This sported the centerpiece—a clear plastic pitcher, filled with plain water, no lemon slice, no ice, and a short stack of Styrofoam cups. She couldn't help thinking, *Oh, we're real high-class here, folks!* Only a single, small window offered redemption.

Unfortunately, Mr. Griffin motioned for Ryons to sit with her back to it. For her, this lifeless environment qualified as the equivalent of someplace like the lobby of a Motel *Negative* 6 in a Twilight Zone episode. She hoped the meeting wouldn't take too long.

Mr. Griffin arrived with a laptop, but also with an assistant whom she'd never seen before. The two men stood facing her. The other man, a stocky six-foot three or so, stood absolutely straight. He came well-suited, wore shiny black shoes, bore no name tag, a fresh crew cut, no facial hair, but did smell of an appealing cologne.

Ryons grumbled to herself, *Obviously, he is one of those humorless, all business types. I bet he won't even drink a drop of water—no matter how long this meeting takes!*

Mr. Griffin exhaled unpleasant, stale coffee breath. His clothes reeked of cigarette smoke and his thinning hair needed tending. *Even a quick one-through with a comb would bring him up a notch… one big notch.*

He said, "Dr. Ryons, Chief of Forensics, this is Johnson. He'll be sitting in on the briefing." Without expression Johnson looked Lissa over, but did not extend a hand in greeting.

Lissa eyed him and did not like his inclusion in the meeting. *Why couldn't I bring an 'assistant,' like Lars?* She also considered, *Yeah! 'Johnson,' that's a real original cover name, alright.*

They all sat down.

Griffin offered, "Think of Johnson here as multi-faceted, multi-talented … well-connected asset or ahh … some such thing— whatever you need to feel comfy in that very intelligent head of yours, Doctor. Just know that he's on our side."

With that out of the way, from a briefcase Johnson pulled out a laptop and opened it. His machine looked like one you couldn't get out of the Dell catalogue—at least not for a few years yet. She was impressed.

Don Griffin continued. "We want to hear your report on the mysterious cloth." Then his tone changed to one of reckless challenge. "Frankly, what the hell is it?" He was being flat-out honest; this caught her unexpectedly. Staring hard, he asked, "And what's this glow shit, huh?"

His professionalism sure slid aside. She blinked and blushed—but not due to his language. She wrongly assumed that the satisfying answers, if there were any, would be coming from his side of the table.

Unruffled, Johnson began navigating on his laptop and doing a little typing.

After going blank for a second or two, Dr. Ryons got back to focusing on the purpose of the meeting. She took out a pad of paper and a pen. Trying to decide where to begin answering, she thought, *Any where … and any way, I guess. Huh, guys?*

First, Lissa thought to sum up the success of the Internet trawling; and then explain how the monitored Napkin Doodling art exhibit had been doing and the intel gathered there, finally the information received from the attempts to date the object by the outside sources. *But wait…what! Did he say "glow?"*

She opened her mouth and began drawing breath to utter her opening line.

Griffin, apparently unable to keep his mouth shut, boldly stated, "We think the napkin was a plant. Someone deliberately snuck it into the Archives Department and left it on the floor near the lost and found…to be found!" He took a short breath. "Either it's a weirdo hoax by somebody with way too much time to spend on their smart little schemes…." Here he paused, regained himself, and with a stern look at Lissa said, "Possibly this enigma is a bizarre artifact from mankind's ancient history or something more from a science-fiction movie, an item due to a paranormal glitch from a different time and dimension. Or, last guess, strange as it sounds, an alien relic—meaning, something that fits in absolutely nowhere…." His voice trailed off. Red in the face, obviously off kilter, sweating, he mumbled, "I know, I must sound like an idiot!"

His impassioned speech did create this presumption in Dr. Ryons. *So, this is how a misfit, grown man not suited for the job behaves when he's unable to solve an out-of-his-league problem!*

Whatever prestige Don Griffin originally walked into the meeting with, completely disintegrated, leaving an air of professionalism diced with stupidity. He squirmed in his seat while fixing his gaze at the ceiling. After several seconds and exhaling a gust of air, he regained his flimsy self-control and squinted at the doctor with a look which she perceived as *Now tell us what we don't know!*

Johnson stopped fooling with his tech toy, and stared at each of them in turn. He then closed the lid. Expressionless, he unmistakably soaked in the moment.

Dr. Ryons was dumbfounded. She pondered, *Did I enter the U.N. building this morning? Yes, I did. Punched in… that was me… I'm NOT dreaming. No, not daydreaming either.* Odd feelings of disorientation shook her. Her thinking became a blur, reminding her of the medicated state experienced while recuperating in the hospital. *I wonder, what the… did he mean an object, wait a minute… which arrived on our earth—via a 'time warp'. Whaaat? Helloou, this is way beyond weird!*

Her elbows rested on the table top. Placing her hands together she unconsciously interlaced her fingers and squeezed. Bewildered, she slightly cocked her head and was about to say just what she wasn't sure, when Johnson spoke.

Johnson stood up. "Grif, step outside in the hall with me for a moment."

Ryons noticed once again how imposing of a figure he made. She also felt that he had arrived with the backing of a large and powerful entity. Don Griffin dutifully followed him out the door like a deflated, bent over, shuffling necessity.

One thing Lissa did know—if she only knew how long they would be out of the room, she wouldn't have hesitated to race over and lift the lid to Johnson's computer and see what he had been doing. *Or not,* she thought. Though Griffin's laptop lid remained up she had no incentive to investigate his.

While waiting, she remained seated on, to her mind, the most un-ergonomically designed chair imaginable. She felt constant pressure like a jabbing against her spine, lower back, thighs, plus the back of her knees twitched fruitlessly. *What I need now is to go downstairs and get a good, hot Chamomile Shuffle then come back to this luxurious meeting room.* A Chamomile Shuffle was her favorite drink which she occasionally had sent up to the lab from the commissary's espresso bar. It contained herbal tea, with a slice of lemon, dash of cinnamon and a hint of chai. Caffeine didn't agree with her so she leaned on herbal tea to get herself right in the head. This meeting already over-qualified for her comfort drink. She impatiently, kept her bottom in her chair.

The men returned a few moments later.

Johnson sat down, looked her way and apologized with a faint grin, "Sorry about that, Doctor Ryons." He opened his laptop again and stared at who-knew-what. Don Griffin, with a bit of squirming settled into his chair. His emotional and professional vulnerability marked by blurting out 'tell me what you know' seemed in check. He now introduced a kind of back-in-charge attitude with the non-combatant body language. Smiling broadly at Dr. Ryons, he clasped his hands as though squeezing the juice out of a challenging piece of fruit. He adjusted his laptop's position on the table as though trying to find the correct mathematical location to the room's architecture. His fidgeting feet crossed and uncrossed at the ankles. With a facial expression representing regard, and with an upbeat outlook, he said, "So, Doctor Ryons, please tell us what you know about the item in question?"

The meeting seemed back to order.

But as she began, he interrupted, raised a hand, and gently started to announce something.

Ryons' eyes took a half-roll, she wondered if he and Johnson would need to take a time-out in the hallway once again.

"Doctor Ryons, if you didn't get the memo," he said with a slight smirk, "the project has an official title. One of the boys in Linguistics typed in the request for a name from some fancy-smancy computer program that spits out random titles. As you know, this is standard procedure for studies, dossiers, Secret or Top Secret files and that sort of thing. I gave my approval, so we have Project Skedaddle before us. It's not quite as weird as some project titles like 'Jelly Dip' or 'Skunk Patrol,' but it'll do."

Smiling, he looked at Johnson and keenly observed a stone face. This caused Griffin's speech to speed up and get out whatever other information he felt imperative to share. "A few days after the official christening, I was notified about an anomaly. I'll tell you something strange. But, it's obviously nothing but...sheer coincidence."

Ryons could see by his shifting squirm that Griffin was uncomfortable with this news.

"One word the linguists believe they have decoded from the napkin's doodles is just that, 'skedaddle,'" he said with a nervous grin and wave-of his hand, as if he successfully re-directed an annoying flying insect.

"To help still your curi…er, well…never mind. Probably it would just stir up that professional curiosity of yours anyway. We let it pass as indeed nothing more than one of life's mildly interesting coincidental glitches…the name, I mean." Griffin half-turned to Johnson and then stopped, having wisely changed his mind.

What he said didn't stir up any curiosity at all. She involuntarily nodded in vague acknowledgement. But, Dr. Ryons did wonder if he'd finally shut up. She decided to allow time to pass. Silently and slowly, she counted to five before she would begin her report. *Okay*, she thought, *here it goes…*. "Several months have passed since Project Skedaddle initiated," she said the word with a grin. "The janitor who found the object has been cleared of any direct or creative knowledge of its origins or purposes."

Don Griffin's mouth began to move, but Johnson put his hand on Griffin's forearm and that was that; Griffin's mouth closed tight.

Lissa thought, *Jeez, how dang important is this Skedaddle thing after all?* "Continuing, the U.N.'s website, specifically set up to funnel tips and information, turned out to be a smart idea!" *A smart one of mine,* she wanted to add. "The website's traffic and potential contributions have been trickling in sporadically. We have registered more than 14,000 hits. There have been interesting comments; professional inquiries and a surplus of teenage boy geek speak pseudo-wisdom—mostly worthy of deletion. You might say that on the Internet there's a squeaky hard drive born every minute. *Yes, I just made it up, and it got no chuckles, not a one!*

"The IT input, in conjunction with the diagram enlargements on exhibit in the lobbies saw certain educated and obviously *degreed* guesses. These solidified into some surprising facts." She stared at both of them and repeated, "Yes, facts. Plus, more than plenty of ideas similar to those you might hear on any given night on the popular, late night, talk-radio show, *Coast to Coast AM.*"

Both men displayed shrugs of ignorance.

"It's an audio melting pot for all things on the fringe. Such as metaphysics, conspiracy theories, UFOs, ghosts, unexplained phenomena. The news and the loons hold equal sway."

The men looked at each other and made notes on paper pads which they now produced. This notating surprised her, so she added, "This show is broadcast nationwide on over 400 affiliate stations and it's been on the air for over 20 years." She thought, *They'll probably just Google it later… or when I turn my back for a second.*

Don Griffin interjected, "At Linguistics, we concluded it's doubtful there's a message of immediate importance, whether it's written in a foreign, ancient or the extreme hypothesis—an alien language." He said this with a nod to both. "Though the writings and finely detailed drawings may be interesting and highly irregular, we see no threat to local, national or global security so far. My code breakers have come up with little aside from 'skedaddle.' The reason it was planted here at this time is unknown." He cleared his throat. "Which I might add has begun affecting our annual research budget."

On that last remark, Ryons put on her stony face.

It was her turn again. "The forensics team arrived at certain suppositions: especially after the dating results came in from the four out-sourced labs. Plus, minor input from creative out-of-the-box thinkers in other departments, mixed with bright ideas of my own." She said the ending with a whimsical, shy smile. The men stared, waiting. The stage was hers alone.

Lissa turned her laptop screen around to show them a split screen of two sets of images which she prepared for their viewing. "This side, your left, shows photographs available from many sites on the Web or in printed publications." She clicked so the two sets of pictures started on a slow loop. There were six per side, twelve in all. Each side displayed drawings, plus the scribblings of a language.

Then she pointed to their right side rotating six images from the cloth, now named Skedaddle. She suppressed a mild bit of humor concerning the odd name associated with weeks of brainstorming, hard work, daydreaming and stress. *Skedaddle? Yeah.*

"As you can see, there are obvious similarities with the two sets: drawings, a handwritten language, and of course the colored stains. The men dutifully nodded. She amused herself, *Of course, they're nodding. Who wouldn't?* She added, "Take a minute and study the samplings of Skedaddle and the other source."

Johnson interjected, "I believe I can make out a word or two on Source B," as he coined it. "Also, some of the sketches seem vaguely conventional, too. Now, I'm curious, Doctor!"

Dr. Ryons was glad to get anything out of that sturdy, poker face. She paused a second or two for emphasis and said, "Source B, as you call it, is photographs of scraps of paper, sheets of paper, fabric napkins and handkerchiefs. The author of all the markings is none other than Albert Einstein! The language is German, that's why a word or two looked familiar to you ah…Mister Johnson.

The doodles on one of the samples are Einstein's theory of the formation of black holes. Another series deals with atoms and their division. There's a Burgundy wine stain on one, coffee on another and even red lipstick on more than one of his unconventional Post-It notes. She applied an educator sound to her voice in finalizing her point, adding, "Jotting down ideas, concepts or even reminders to buy milk on anything handy such as a cloth napkin are nothing new. Science and groceries can meet equally on a scrap of paper, gentlemen."

Griffin slapped his hands on the table, grinned and fairly shouted, "That solves it, by Jove! So, Albert's our man!"

The other two simply stared and let the uneasy moment pass. But, in his mock joviality, he outspread both arms and pushed back his chair away from the table with a face befriending amazement. Unfortunately, in his exertion, he tilted his weight too much and started falling backwards.

Without so much as a glance, Johnson caught the back of Griffin's chair and righted it as if it took no thought or strength to accomplish the save. Don Griffin's head twaddled as his body stabilized. After a few short breaths, he put his reddened face down and managed to eke out a faint, "Let's continue, Doctor."

At this point, Lissa thought, *Hell with it! A long strange meeting is at hand.* She decided to text the espresso bar, The United Libations, ordering her Shuffle. After the phone call ended, her fingernails danced on the tabletop. She could guess what both Griffin and Johnson thought by their grinning faces, *Very good research, confounding… creative!* Neither said anything.

Pleased with herself, she turned the screen back around and set about choosing which direction to proceed. Divining by their previous reaction or their lack thereof, made her decide to leave the dating results for last. *They can sit on their asses and wait for that!*

But to them she said, "Alright, gents!" They visibly perked up at this. *Good!*

"The data volunteered from astronomers, mathematicians and astrophysicists funneling through our websites and the exhibit, surprised us. The largest sketch on the napkin, meticulously done, like all of them … to ahh, put it in the vernacular, was just a bitch to decipher. But when all the test determinations arrived from our third parties, they astounded my team. I too, found myself astounded!"

At that point a knock on the door broke her enthusiasm. Tea delivery. Lissa popped the lid off and gratefully savored the aroma. She blew across the surface of the steaming drink and sipped. Her stressed, professional exterior relaxed.

The commissary delivery person looked at the two men and with a perky smile. Hospitably he enthusiastically asked, "Will you gentlemen be ordering anything? The Libations' muffins are r-e-a-l-l-y good today! I can make it back here right quick, no problemo! Yessiree."

Flicking a hand, a terse, shoo-away tone came out of Johnson. Without eye contact, he answered for Griffin and himself, "No and good-bye!" Griffin let out, what could only be interpreted as a whimper. Apparently, the muffins caught his tummy's attention.

They were alone again, three grown-ups, three computers and one provocative theme.

Chapter 22

Setting the paper cup aside, Lissa turned her screen around to show one scan of a section of the napkin. Then after a click, zoomed-in, revealing perhaps 30 dots, tiny swirls and blurs in black, on a stark white background. She began, "Like all of the scans, the graphics personnel cleaned them up in Photoshop. Then one of the graphic artists had an interesting idea...flip the image by reversing the colors. The positive image became a negative. The contrast added significant definition. Simply put, white became black and the doodle dots white. This turned a very big corner for all of us. Our collective assumptions of a representation of the nighttime sky solidified. The image depicted stars, but mainly galaxies; different styles of them: spiral, elliptical, clusters, etc. When we opened the files at the lab all of us let out a combined sigh of relief and knew we were on our way—somewhere.

"So, we pursued astronomers who had already volunteered input and also the resources they recommended. But none of the digital images from NASA gathered from the Hubble Space Telescope resembled this view of the night sky. Many hours went into looking for this needle in the celestial haystack. The limited availability of such photographs and star charts converted into software were disappointing. No one wanted to make a career out of the napkin caper.

"Those at the U.N., working with me on Project Skedaddle held out only a faint hope of finding a match from what the astronomical sciences compiled. It goes without saying that the celestial arena is infinitely vast. Many man hours were spent on this search, making our efforts begin to feel plain old stupid. Also, we often wondered what could be so important about this star field anyway. These searches really puzzled the best of the best, until computerized star charts of the heavens in 360 degrees and in 3-D became available. Any questions so far?" There were none; she had their attention now. Ryons picked up her cup and sipped, enjoying her reliable but silent, tasty friend.

"Then about two weeks ago, shortly after the exhibit started here in the Tower, in walks Professor Luc Sigurdsson. He's an astronomer visiting from Luxembourg. He happened to be in New York for a conference and came to the U.N. like any other tourist. The Napkin Doodling exhibit intrigued him. I need to point out that before the graphic artist's idea to reverse the white to black all 42 digital prints were completed. But, we've updated the website. Okay?

"I interviewed the security guard later that day. He filled me in on this visitor's behavior before I arrived. After a long time of viewing, this man pulled out a hand-held, micro-computer, took photos and entered data. He sat down on a nearby couch totally absorbed by the exhibit. After a quarter of an hour he got up to view more of the images. Professor Sigurdsson took several more photos of the designs and sat back down again, concentrating on his computer.

"Apparently he stared at the 14 images; obviously calculating in deep contemplation. I might add that in all of our surveillance of the three identical exhibits, rarely did anyone take photos. This man was the most interested party we came across.

"Just when it appeared he might exit the building, he veered over to this same security guard to ask him a question. This caught our attention."

He said, "'Excuse me officer, since when is the United Nations so interested in astronomy? Don't we have enough problems to solve down here on this planet? What a waste of humanitarian aid paying the 'doodler,' then enlarging and framing these pictures? Why has the U.N. invested in head scratching doo-dles? He took off his hat and using his fingers he scratched his head and said, 'Doo-dles' in a slow mocking tone. Who proposed this comic relief?

"The security guard's eyes went large and round. He told me later that his body felt like he received a mild electric shock, making little snap-snap sounds in his clothing."

Johnson interjected, "Like static electricity."

Ryons nodded. "But more so." She continued. "In his nearly three weeks of tending the exhibits this security guard heard everything from how the 'art' money should have been spent to feed starving orphans, how cool the exhibit was, and far too many ludicrous, theoretical interpretations. But this was the first visitor to inquire as to who he might talk to about this strange 'art' exhibit.

"BINGO! That's when this all turned an unexpected second corner for us, and I do mean unexpected." She paused, took a few sips of her now cooled drink and let the cheap elixir sink in before beginning again.

The two men leaned in, as if doing so would help them hear better. "The security guard directed Professor Sigurdsson to the receptionist to whom he gave his business card and explained why. Unfortunately, this was a floater employee from another floor. No one informed this person of the protocol for this exhibit.

"But, merely taking his card, with assurances to pass it along to the proper persons wasn't good enough for our gray-haired visitor. Apparently, he wasn't going to slip through a crack which he perceived lay before him. The security guard noticed Professor Sigurdsson's annoyance. The old man's hands slapped down on the counter. A rising, irritated, European accent added to his

The Drop

leaning posture which frightened the seated employee. So, the guard returned, attempting to be as helpful as possible.

"After a quick interview, the guard sized-up Professor Sigurdsson to be the real thing—a person with answers—and not another hard-headed or soft-hearted, money-conscious crank or an escapee from a mental institution. He phoned the Forensics Department.

"I made impromptu plans as quick as I could to meet this professor in the commissary of the Visitor's Center. Leaving my lab coat behind, I so-to-speak, put on my exhibition curator hat.

"When I met him, I saw a well-dressed, nicely mannered, gentleman in his mid-sixties. White mustache, glasses, and a peach colored rose in his lapel. In a few minutes I judged him passionate with his opinions, which he expressed in fairly good, accented English. I remember he had on a quaint, burgundy bow tie. He slung an overcoat on an arm, under which he clutched U.N. topical Fact Sheets, a variety of brochures, and thin publications published by the U.N. Department of Public Information. I suggested he place his belongings with the guard, and he did.

"When we greeted and shook hands he took off his hat which sported a white feather on one side. I remember his very warm hands." She decided not to add that he had on cologne which she had never smelled before, but which truly captivated her senses.

"I did have a practiced script for such a meeting, if ever one was to take place. But, most of it drained away as he did most of the talking. I introduced myself only as Lissa Ryons from the PR department. Before I left the lab, I put on my accompanying false name tag.

"After introductions and small talk, he quizzed me about the exhibits' origins and content and purpose. We decided to go have a close look at the images together. His first question surprised me.

129

With outstretched arms he emphatically asked "'Why are there fairies mixed in with sketches of outer space?'"

"Confusion showed in his face and his voice strained when he added, 'Why has the United Nations spotlighted what must be absolute visual gibberish to all of you? You, I ask you why?" He pointed to one picture. "Here you have highly-advanced, mathematical equations, physics' questions, with the answers in an esoteric looking language, and these mixed together with precise renderings of distances between key galaxies, plus possible conclusions about String Theory, and then fairies floating about. Are fools and geniuses working together on the U.N. payroll, is that what's taken place Miss Ryons? Again I ask you?'"

"He leaned toward me and slid his eye glasses down his nose. Mr. Sigurdsson stared right at me and repeated, 'Hmm?' He remained fixed that way waiting for an answer."

Dr. Ryons paused; both Griffin and Johnson exchanged smirks then gawked at her. At the same time, both said, "Fairies?"

Don Griffin remarked, "You mean, like fairy tale fairies; elves, witches and all that?"

"Yep! That's right, gentlemen, you got it." She let that settle in while taking the last sip of her drink. "So Professor Sigurdsson, with that stare of his, continued to lean, and almost made me jump when he reiterated in a commanding tone, 'Hmm?' He stood firm and peered at me looking genuinely perplexed. He knew he had me.

"I stood there perplexed. I don't know how many seconds passed, but I felt like I had met more than my match and gone down on the first punch.

"He eased his body up and stood straight. So, without a clue as to which way to take this, I proposed that if he had the time, would he please tell me his—and here I had to chose between interpretation or understanding, and I went with the latter—his understanding of the images.

"Professor Sigurdsson, as it turns out, is a university professor and he teaches astrophysics in Europe. Just the kind of visitor we'd been waiting, hoping and praying for.

"He pointed out what he meant. Indeed, on the napkin there were small but anatomically correct drawings of two naked humans: one male, one female. Gentlemen, we will now reference that area as Skedaddle Section 12. On Skedaddle Section number 6, there is one creature almost identical to the humans but obviously and peculiarly, on its back are two large wings. It is true there are several winged 'fairy' like characters on the Skedaddle document. They are slightly larger than the nude male and female, but are clothed and bearing weapons."

"Weapons?" Both Griffin and Johnson remarked. Again, they leaned in with interest.

"Yes, swords," Lissa answered.

"Ahh … c'mon, doc. You're losing me." Griffin said, with a now familiar smirk.

"Hold on. I wasn't sure how to respond to this highly educated man. Remember, guys, where he calls 'home.' European mythology, like the Brothers' Grimm for example, is a centuries-old, oral tradition of tales. Here, we call them bedtime stories. Even today in places like Iceland, a significant portion of the population believes that elves and trolls still live in the mountains and fields. Oh! I forgot—he also pointed at the enlarged coffee stains that are on Sections 2, 5 and 10 and commented, 'What the heck are these brown blotches, some sort of abstract artistic statement for those of low class, little minds and no taste?'

"Sneering, he added, 'Looks like a stein splash from last Oktoberfest!' After that criticism, he snorted and flapped his arms many times, like a bird. 'Look I am a drunken fairy everyone! Oh my, I'm a fairy who's had his fill.' He was not smiling.

"A little embarrassed I looked around, but the lobby was nearly empty. I let the outburst pass." In the small meeting room, Lissa looked at her silent audience of two unflappable men. She could see that they were waiting for something more substantial.

"We spent an hour or more chatting, interrupted by a few calls and text messages on his cell phone. I thought, 'Apparently, he's a busy man.' The Professor spoke in a language not close to any European ones which I had familiarity. We made our way back to the commissary from the exhibit.

"So, here's that 'big corner' that I mentioned. And it's amazing!" She grinned and began her downhill course of data.

"By the way, it didn't take him long to figure out that I was too educated to be just an art curator or PR person. I didn't expose any more than I felt I had to, but he said, 'I can recognize a fellow scientist when I meet one, Miss Ryons.' I kept quiet, being answer enough for him."

Johnson impatiently prodded her, "And the next big corner, *please Doctor!*"

Enthusiastically, she continued, "First, the Professor's eyes shined, filling with liquid, almost, but not quite tears. That caught my attention. What was coming, I couldn't remotely guess.

"He urged me to take a good long look at Section 3. He explained that it was, of course 'an astronomical...' he searched for the right English word, 'schematic.' He said that it wasn't the 'view of the nighttime sky we surmised it to be.' Adding emphasis he said, 'Whatever you and your team have come up with is wrong! The viewpoint, the point of origin, is not from the planet we are standing on.'

"That was a shock, and not just intellectually. I literally felt it run through my entire body. I cocked my head and looked him over from his dark green leather shoes to the dapper hat on his head. No, he wasn't a weirdo, not a kook. At least I didn't want him to be one! Also, he said 'your team,' now where did he get that from?

"As I stared at him, he must have read my mind and said, 'I know it sounds ludicrous…believe me. You think me a reckless buffoon, no doubt!' He recommended in a half-quirky, half-serious way, with a tight smile also thrown in; that we 'take our computer image and reverse it on the monitor and view it from the opposite direction. He suggested we should turn it around and see where it takes us.'"

She said to the men, with her hands flat on the table and mildly shaking her head sideways, "A light bulb was not glowing above my head, not yet...but it was coming. He hooked my curiosity—deep curiosity, that's for sure.

"The Professor said, 'Miss Ryons, I assume you must have come up empty, if you have not, then you will. I have no doubt about that! This view is not one seen from Earth. The view is looking toward the Earth. Flip your galaxies around and through them you will see where we stand right now. This beautiful spaceship called Earth is the very speck, centered in the middle of this area of the napkin-turned-sky chart. This map of the heavens is from the perspective of a location in outer space. It is accurate in its exactness of, how do you say it in English…light year distances; at least to the extent they can be represented on a napkin by someone who is drinking coffee, mind you.'

"He added, 'Use that innovative Hubble Reckoning 3-D software that NASA and the military don't want you to know about yet. After you reverse your sky chart, set up the location perspective directly above the Earth's Arctic region, placing it near the current North Pole. Then go backward from the schematic's view. Proceed searching until the Earth arrives in the center."

Almost in a whisper she said to the men, "I pondered that. This was, and still is, a lot to take in. If he could read my thoughts or simply my facial expressions, he saw the need to clarify the meaning.

"He continued his explanation. 'When you pursue getting your 3-D image properly coordinated with the Pole, you will need to turn back the clock to synchronize when the evening sky appeared exactly the way it is noted here on this section.'

"In a jesting tone, as if there was anything to joke about, he added, 'It might make you a little cuckoo going backwards on the calendar until the celestial objects match the picture. It's more than just a few years ago, mind you, Miss Ryons.' His face beamed and he nodded slightly seeing if I followed his emphasis.

"To top it off he walked me to Section 4 and pointed at one diagram. With little emotion and a faint smile, said, 'You know or perhaps you did not, this is the shape of your universe.' He looked at me as if he had solved a very strange and extraordinary riddle.

"I thought that due to translating his thoughts into English from his native tongue he innocently mixed up, 'our' with 'your.' So, I left it alone.

"I stood half mystified, half boggled, with a pinch of sobriety and an appetite for more puzzle master talk. But, he said that he had a flight to catch and 'used up' the last of his sightseeing time here at the U.N. with me. Then he made a slight bow and left."

"When he exited, I sensed the vast emptiness of the lobby. All the oxygen took on a precise amount of cubic feet and weight; the height to the ceiling; the square footage of the floor, distances between the four walls, window thickness, light bulb wattages, carpet density, all knowable, logical, mathematical truths. All discernible by conventional methodical equations. The calculations danced in my imagination—but I didn't need a calculator."

She paused, and looked at the plain wall ahead of her but not really seeing anything. She gulped and continued. "Strange, yes. These numbers and coordinates became attractive to me. Every day, such locations hold facts, wherever we are. But even this sterile room has a life or purpose, defined by math. An architect designs, contractors build, we inhabit. Where ever I go, I can't help but distill more and more of the innate knowledge which all five senses are analyzing. Every waking moment, data is basting each one of us." She ended with a far off look.

The doctor had spoken with confidence, perceptively moving the two men off kilter. At a loss for comment, silence followed. The two listeners turned to each other. Neither face had any expression. After a moment, each raised their heads to eye the blank ceiling and then look over the bare walls and floor. Their minds must have been equally empty, not knowing what to say.

Shrugging his head and shoulders as if a chill passed through him, Don Griffin broke the thickening silence. "Wow! What a tale. What a guy to have…ahh…um, met. What luck or 'Luc' I mean!" Griffin looked proud of his wit.

Lissa guessed Griffin had been sitting on this pun waiting for the instant he could use it.

Chapter 23

As if on cue, Johnson turned his laptop screen around, revealing a large image of, as he called him, "Luc, the man from Luxembourg." In this photograph, Professor Sigurdsson was carefully examining one of the framed diagrams. The close up shot of the Professor showed him staring straight ahead with a small portion of Lissa's face behind him.

This caught her attention. Annoyance lacing her words, she asked, "How did you get … take … that, photo from that perspective? At these exhibits, I thought only audio devices and the lobby's ceiling mounted surveillance cameras were utilized?"

Johnson ignored her questions. He spoke with a flat, dry expression. "Dr. Ryons, the man you were chumming it up with, was no Carl Sagan, although he wanted you to think so." Then he looked around the conference room, obviously deciding where next to take this meeting. He knew he had baited her. His sober-face plainly held a coming pronouncement; an emotion-squashing yank of a hook into its perfect location.

But Griffin interjected, "Doc, there's way more to this man than you'll be comfortable knowing."

Lissa smiled and folded her arms. "Oh, like he was a hologram, or he was beamed up after he left the building?" Her memories of Professor Sigurdsson were warm and extraordinary. She didn't like him being made fun of. "I think he's smarter than if both of you were put in a blender and set to 'Semi-Smart Human.'"

"Ouch! That hurt!" Griffin cooed, rubbing one hand like a hurting paw, and a pained face for full effect. With feigned pomposity he added, "Johnson, I thought you said a Crop Circle swallowed him up?"

By his listeners' rolling eyes, it was apparent they knew this rhetorical question made no sense. Griffin was at his finest worst.

Lissa guessed that Griffin felt even less intelligent by the way he quickly switched to look down at his computer. He turned red and wiped at beads of perspiration on his forehead.

Johnson said with a huff, "Griffin, a way of shutting you up is unfortunately something technology hasn't invented yet!" Then he looked at Lissa. "Speaking of technology, let's get to the dating of that very clever napkin."

Apparently, Griffin wasn't going to let that criticism pass without a cheap fling. After a grim smile at Johnson he spat out, "You D.O.D. types can be real asses too, y' know!"

Unruffled, Johnson shot back, "At least Grif, you know you are one! Thanks for reassuring us though."

Lissa stared at what looked like two quarreling boys in men's bodies. They certainly were an odd pair.

So, Johnson works for the Department of Defense; that explained some things. But, why did the U.N. get the military involved? I've never liked personnel employed by three-letter government agencies, the I.R.S. especially. And what qualifications did Griffin have that facilitated him to wear that suit and be on the U.N. payroll? What a genuine jerk.

Lissa closed her eyes in dismay and blew air out of her puckering lips. Then, she gave them a bored expression which included a fake yawn and droopy eyes. Her attempt at traditional throat clearing turned their attention back to her. In hopes of restarting the professionalism of the meeting, and seeing that the classic segue cue brought them closer to business, Lissa cleared her throat again. Now, the two men appeared calm.

With finality in her voice, she mused, "Done yet, boys? Kinda bumpy in here?" She regretted her earlier, indignant words but was willing to forget them if the men did, too.

Beginning again, she said, "The findings of the four outside sources revealed that the age of the cloth— "

Griffin broke in. Grinning, with unexpected leverage, he said with a sneer, "Was that it's too damn f'n old!" He folded his arms, proud of himself once again. He leaned back in his chair, but cautiously this time. He looked to Lissa with a Beat That! expression.

Lissa clarified, "Not exactly stated in those words, but it does sum them up, no pun intended!" She couldn't help throw that in. Her belief was that if a pun can be punned, one had a duty to not pass it up. It went over their heads without the tiniest bit of recognition.

She queried Griffin, "And how did you guess my answer would be that the specimen was dated as extremely old?" He only smirked, contributing nothing.

Johnson surprised her, beginning to spout. *That's the only word that fits the demeanor*, she thought. *Now it's his turn to dump some more on me.*

He read from his laptop, "Radiocarbon dating, cosmo-chemistry, isochronal rubidium-strontium techniques, carbon dating—14, accelerator mass spectrometry, Argon-argon, Lead-lead, radioactive isotopes, isotopic fractionation and concentrations, ol' Mr. Doppler's shiftiness of measuring photospheric absorption lines, radiometrics, Hubble's Law, density parameters…oh and did I mention accelerator mass spectrometry and all those dainty little neutrons spinning around? Did I leave anything out, Doctor?" He finished with a smug seriousness, tilted his head and stared at her, arms folded.

Red, her pulse raced. Jaw muscles ached as she bit down hard.

Damn him! He's hacked into my files and read the entire report no doubt! What a nasty side this man has. This whole time he's known what I would say. Both of them… have known? Damn, damn. But… why the meeting? Goons.

To answer his rhetorical question, in a voice tinged with embarrassment and spite, Dr. Ryons said, "Yes, you forgot one thing—eons of time!" *What a jackass! I hold out little hope for whatever marriage he might currently be in.*

Don Griffin turned to Johnson and nervously said, "You really know all this scientific shit about time stamping and chemical signatures?"

Johnson didn't bother to answer; he just looked at Lissa while his tongue pushed out one of his cheeks. He was playing a game, and enjoyed the card trick he pulled.

Feeling pinned down; Lissa thought she'd shake things up and send out a probe. "Johnson, what is this peculiarity about Professor Sigurdsson that you and Griffin inferred?"

"It's good you're sitting down for this. He's a strange bird who helped hatch something foul. No pun intended." Johnson paused, obviously searching how to really display his knowledge. He chose to speak with an air of superiority—apparently a favorite.

Lissa thought, *Oh, p-l-e-a-s-e! No, don't give me that know-it-all BS attitude! I don't get paid enough for this benign won't-you-please-dumb-it-down-for-me business!* To her surprise, when he did speak, those thoughts vanished.

"Our very intelligent friend, Luc from Luxembourg, is nowhere to be found in Europe, especially the Grand Duchy of Luxembourg. We circulated his photo to other, quote, 'astrophysicists' over there. No one knows the dear Professor. Remember Luc left this inventive personal calling card?" Johnson then pulled the card out of his shirt pocket and placed it on the table for them to inspect.

With resentment, Lissa thought, *Damn! How did he get that out of my locked file cabinet?* She groaned inside. Feeling like a little girl before a playground bully, Johnson aroused insecurities long unfelt. She sensed her professional, well-earned pride diminishing.

He continued. "Luc, master of deception, or is he simply one of those fascinating fairies—minus the wings and sword of course? The phone number on the card doesn't exist, nor the address, nor apparently the man." He let this bounce around the room for a few seconds before adding, "My people checked listings for local conferences during the window of dates that he was visiting our fair city. No scientific seminars of any sort, nothing in a hundred-mile radius. Sorry Doctor." He paused and then with a slight mocking in his voice, added, "But in the thriving township of Elmsford, some miles to the north, there was a stamp collecting conference. Y'know, finger lickin', sticky Philatelic stuff." His eyes took on the appeal of a lone, dead fish. Glancing at his laptop he clicked, noting, "VFW Hall."

His smirk lived and died an all too memorable fade.

Lissa did not like his smugness. The walls of the room moved closer, squeezing into a disorienting stifling grip. Scared, she wanted to resist this personal attack of her credibility. Lifeless seconds clicked. Overwhelmed, her thinking stopped. Lissa passed into a stunned state of mind, quite unaware of her surroundings. In a deeply rooted human survival skill, she shut down. The veteran analytical capacity hit an unexpected wall. Now she lay debilitated in worthless pieces. *'… nor apparently the man.'*? She choked and reached for water.

Don Griffin played another disturbing card. "Doctor, in the commissary while you were having your get to know each other time, you two weren't alone … not at all. An associate of Johnson's, a suit with a laptop, setup shop there—you might have noticed him? Well, this agent's fancy-schmancy laptop housed a hypersensitive, directional micro-listening device for spying on you and the fairyman."

That comical title irritated her so deeply. She wanted to glare at him but forgot the motor mechanisms needed to do such a maneuver. The alarm in her heart superseded everything else.

"Now, Doc you can't be upset by our spying and secrecy. It's all in the very fine print of the contract you signed when you took this job with us three years ago. Anyway, Johnson's agent supplied Linguistics with pretty good voice recordings of Luc's phone conversations." He paused long and smirked steadily. "Do you wanna take a guess what my language experts heard?"

Lissa felt like a caged pet about to be fed food that was wrong for its diet but the owner was too dumb to know or care. *Eat this?* She fidgeted with the laptop in front of her, eyes stared at the wall and her feet tapped.

"Doc, I'll tell yah…all gibberish, just pure gibberish. Nonsensical, mean anything to you? Anyway, it didn't match anything in our vast recordings of known languages—got it? Not one sentence. We even shopped the recordings around to affiliates in Europe, the Far East and Latin America. Zip! He was fruit cakin' yah! The man was not talkin' to anybody on this planet with those phony phone calls. Oh, 'so busy.' Oh yeah, me too! I bet he was probably texting a stateside mistress." Griffin finished. Using a fingernail, he picked at a piece of lunch stuck between his teeth.

Being an ass must come natural to him. He most likely doesn't know the difference between when his mouth farts, his butt burps or his mind thinks. But right now, I think I'm caught in his damn tailwind.

Lissa started to come out of her overloaded, empty condition. She heard her own voice saying, "This can't be, you're crazy, you're both nuts! Some cruel joke. Hah! Hah! Back at you guys!" *Goons.* Her armpits oozed enough for warm drops to slide down her sides.

The perspiration on her neck and head went cold and sticky. *Did someone sneak in here and squirt me with a spray bottle of sweat?*

Don Griffin, for all his lack of civility, attempted to allow the head of Forensics to save some face. "Doctor, we know you considered this Luc fellow a Santa Claus of Cosmic Knowledge or something like that, an Illuminator. But what I said is true, bizarre but true. Other than a few facts Johnson told me on the ride up here, all I knew coming into the meeting was that the guy was fishy…something just not kosher about him. The napkin was a prop, a forgery—meaningless. By the way, what was the date again of the Shroud of the U.N.?"

Lissa heard herself mechanically mouth, "All dates came in the billions, 13 billion the highest." Then she stiffly stood up. Speaking in a monotone, she mumbled that she needed to go to the ladies room. Then her flower of the day, a magenta mini-orchid, fell to the carpet. Both men made half-motions toward the loss, not saying anything. The zombie look stopped them.

* * *

Back in the meeting room, the two men talked like men did. "Why the hell does it always take women so long in the bathroom, huh?" Griffin said with a yawn and a chuckle.

"You think she's deciding whether to take the red pill or the blue pill?" Johnson said, referencing the crucial scene with Neo and Morpheus from the movie The Matrix. He continued, "Personally, I think her head's too big to fit down that rabbit hole!" He quickly added, "But not that ass of hers." They both laughed, then quickly glanced at the door.

Griffin asked, "By the way, where the hell is Luxembourg anyway, some suburb of London isn't it?"

Johnson rolled his eyes. "No. It's a tiny country, set betwixt France and Germany. If you're driving and sneeze, you might miss it." Sneering with a far off gaze he added, "I hear it's lovely this time of year!"

Chapter 24

The restroom door closed behind Lissa. She muttered, "What does it all mean? According to science, that's the date of the beginning of the universe!"

She was glad to be the only one in the restroom. Glancing in the mirror, her expression reflected a desperate, aimless stare. One eyelid twitched. Standing at the sink, arms limp, strength near gone, she splashed cold water on her face. But feeling faint she dabbed herself off and kept the damp paper towel in her hand. Lissa put her weight against the nearest wall and slid down until she came to rest on the cold, tiled floor. *I don't give a crap if someone walks in.*

Twisted thoughts grew as she twirled a wet lock of her auburn hair which flopped in her face. Like a person needing fresh air, she gulped for reason and sense. Her eyes stared straight in front of her. Overly lit, shiny bright walls reflected in the porcelain and chrome fixtures. *The achievement of hygienic housecleaning and sterility around-the-clock... is the height of mankind's innovative spirit—sanitation?*

She muttered, "My career just hit the biggest speed bump imaginable, no—unimaginable!"

Lissa kicked herself in an incriminating cycle of questioning. How did she miss putting the pieces together when it was so obvious? *I walked into a trap!* She mumbled, "Lissa, my dear, did that bomb blast blow your head the wrong way... or somthin'? A man, a being, or perhaps... an alien, a criminal or whatever, was up to some mischief using me as a key player, his prey. Then doodled on a napkin while sipping coffee, thousands of light years away, a billion plus years ago and doing what? Designing the universe? Designing humans? Creating Creation? No way!" Lissa shook her head in amazed disbelief.

She hiccupped and began a nervous giggle which tickled her sanity. "This just doesn't make sense. That napkin showed absolutely no decay. That's one damn good napkin! What fabric!" She hiccupped again. "Was that Luc guy, a setup, a schemer or somethin' else? Crap! What a stinker! It's a conspiracy and I'm the fall guy—girl, whatever." Hiccup.

Lissa massaged her temples while she attempted to sort out truth from fiction. "Aside from that, it still glows, how could it? Why would it?" Thoughts raced, tumbled, blossomed and mashed into one another. She see-sawed from barely tethered merriment to absolute discouragement and then back again. Disillusionment pried between the two seeking to claim her for its own.

Is it like those TV ads showing the wonderful moments for sipping the perfect cup of coffee? Or were the moments made wonderful, due to sipping the perfect cup of coffee? Or the perfect mo...ohh. So, God was experiencing a beautiful Big Bang morning moment? I wonder. Is that what this is all about? That's just too stupid to think a Supreme Being would even drink coffee. How big would the cup have to be? Also, that'd probably be the strongest cup of coffee ever made. No, no, no that's crazy talk. Just plain c-r-a-z-y talk. Her thinking broke through walls, norms, and then bounced and trounced on. *I mean the latest studies show that caffeine isn't good for the heart or something... or, is it?*

Her thoughts wandered off into a land of fuzziness where strange, colorful flying creatures from Luxembourg were at home, but she wasn't.

Light-headed, not wanting to stand up, Lissa reached for the sink to wet the paper towel still in her hand. But because of the angle she couldn't manage the maneuver. Instead, she balled it and threw the towel. This stuck on the wall across from her. "Now I've done it." She pronounced, "They can fire me for that … if they like!"

She scrunched up her knees and after a moment let her feet go wide, legs spread out. "Maybe my karma bag is full and that's why this is happening to me. Karma bag—what's that? Where did that come from? Lissa hun, you're startin' to lose it and lose it big time!" She closed her eyes, drew her knees up again and held them tight. "I'm just not that kind of person; I'm an atheist, aren't I? I've never been religious and I don't want to start wasting time on superstitions now. How can I dig my heels into stipulated beliefs that conflict with someone else's stipulated beliefs? Oh boy! What fun. Competing religions, oh yeah! Count me in. I can't wait."

In her view of life and her knowledge of history, God deserved to have the entire human race file a mega, class action lawsuit against him or her for all the endless pain and confusion he either intended or ignored. "He scores very high for lame-ousity. Century after century … are we any better off? Kill, kill. Destroy, destroy. Bomb, bomb. Bomb...me!" She sobbed at the remembrance of being a victim of religious violence. In a flash she relived all the pain and suffering again. Tears ran through her fingers covering her face. She ranted to nobody. Years of disappointment, sorrow and disenchantment welled up and passed through her eyes. A sleeve now served as an absorbent witness, another piece of evidence in her case against the Creator. Angry and dominated by self-pity mixed with delusional rhetoric, Lissa internally kicked at the unseen force which allowed her to think out of the box, but prevented her from getting out of the box, herself.

Never enough unity for us humans, never was, never will be. What a mixed-up species we are. The Not United Nations. That's the reality of it. Why doesn't he just end it all? Or is "it" just watching, waiting for us do it by our lunatic selves? Or, maybe people like those two suits are the real lunatics. Grrr, I can't face those jackasses again! What's that Johnson up to anyway? He's already snooped through my files. Is he trying out new military mind control techniques on me? And that flippin' Griffin, what a goon and a loon. No doubt he's a card carrying Ignoramus. Probably the nephew of some big shot running around here. Did Johnson bring him along for warped comic relief! If so, it worked.

She reflected on the effect of the cloth's luminance on the lab team. "'Pleasant,' Lars said. Meaning, God, Mister Alien, Mister Big Super-Person or Persons—whoever, could be pleasant, too. The Man upstairs. Maybe that's not so bad. Actually, maybe it's good news. So, I'm wonderin' if the luminance had the same result on our D.O.D. idiot, slash agent? He obviously sneaked in the lab after we closed up at night and checked out my office and Skedaddle's progress? Skedaddle? What the hell kind of name is that—a joke?"

Enjoying the privacy, she mumbled on. "And what about our Moon? Is that some glorious mistake, now minus the original glory? What went wrong with that world, reverse pimples? Crippled, battered to hell by a zillion meteors. Not one critter crawlin' around on that rock—what's zup with dat! One of God's failures, under-engineered or sumthin'?"

Like a grown-up leaning down to scold a child, Lissa shook her tired head while wagging an index finger. "Too, too much to process, Lissa babe, you are losin' it. Is there is a GODCHAT.com or a SUPREMEBEING.org out there with all the answers?" She giggled and said, "I better get out of here, those guys probably think I'm either constipated or I fell in."

Using the small of her back and pressing hard on her shoes, Lissa wiggled her way up the tiles. Ending in a slouch, she caught her breath and subdued a moan. "Thoughts. So many thoughts whirling around in this ol' head of mine." Giving into gravity, her fatigued body slid back down. Every thread Lissa pulled on evolved into a crippling lifeline of hope. *I got nothin'.*

"For a short time, my life seemed like I'd unexpectedly received a coupon for huge savings at a fantastic place where I've never shopped before. But now, I've looked at the fine print. The expiration date has passed. And all my hopes for those great deals are at an end, one big ugly, useless end." She stared at the wadded wet cloth stuck on the opposite wall.

A woman entered the ladies restroom. She passed by Lissa without looking at her. Stepping into a toilet stall she closed the door. This motivated Lissa to stand up straight and prepare herself to go back to the conference room of mysteries and the two fools. She glanced in the mirror and winced, *Ahh, my dear, you've seen better days! You look like hell in a lab coat with earrings on. Aww! Where's my flower?* A place in her soul whimpered for the spark of nature's beauty. She looked on the floor and seeing nothing, threw her hands up. *Why do flowers have color anyway? Why is everything in nature so amazing, intricate and beautiful? Could the world be beauty-fuller? There are what, some 250,000 species of flowers in the world—probably not an ugly one in the bunch! But why can people be so attractive and act horrible? Mother Nature is really something, but her ugly step-sister must've spawned the human race.*

She sized up her looks in the reflection. Her upper lip tasted salty from dried tears. *I suppose I should be thankful for my good looks.* She dabbed at her smeared makeup, washed her face, neck and hands. *Damn. Why does every liquid soap dispenser have to smell like heaven is made of vanilla?* She started to tidy up her clothes but then grunted, "Aw, to hell with it!"

Chapter 25

Before she went back into the meeting room, Lissa had an idea. Using her cell phone, she called the lab and asked for Lars. When he answered, Lissa opened the meeting room door and stuck her head in. She held up her cell phone, explaining that she had to, "take this call." She closed the door and walked a short distance down the hall.

"Lars, something has been nagging me which I'd like you to clarify." She exhaled a long slow breath while piecing together the right words.

"Certainly Doctor, how can I help you?"

"Lars, you told me that the crew knew about the luminescent property of the napkin. Afterwards, I imagined that while I convalesced, perhaps the electrical power must have shorted-out during a storm, causing the whole lab to go dark. Or, one of you forgot to put it away and while closing up the lab for the night, discovered the luminescence. When I heard the discovery from you…" Here she paused, searching for words that wouldn't disclose her secrecy or feelings of betrayal from her coworkers. "I was…quite surprised. Yet, I never asked how this came about. I'm curious Lars…what happened, exactly?" She felt that her professionalism survived quite well.

Dr. Ryons couldn't see the whimsical roll of the eyes and twinkle of a smile on the other end of the phone though. Lars thought, *Took her long enough! And the pride that some people try to cover up.*

"Of course Doctor, I will tell you." He considered how best to approach this. "Sorry, if you had any impression of a ... conspiracy to delay or to never tell you. Please believe me. I meant to bring up the matter shortly after you came back to work. Nothing intentional, or purposely kept hidden from you by me. If I remember correctly, you arrived preoccupied with catching up on office duties. Also, the pressure of the Ebola results were demanded from upstairs. So, I let it go until later. We all did. One thing led to another, time simply zipped away. When you meditated on the napkin during breaks ... we ahh ... saw a look in your eyes ...."

He searched for words to correctly describe his memories. "The matter was odd."

'*Odd,*' was the right word, Lissa thought, as she focused on the coming explanation.

"The night before I found out, I had a vivid and realistic dream. I woke as soon as it ended and sat up in bed quite absorbed and animated. This startled my wife, who luckily is a deep sleeper. She says my snoring could raise the sleeping Viking lords at the bottom of the fjords—mind you."

Lissa's voice rose, straining with anxiety. "Lars!"

He heard the impatient groan. "Sorry. As I was saying, I dreamed that I went to work like any other day. I told my wife I had a dream about work, then she gave me a bored looked and fell right back to sleep."

"You dreamed you went to work?" Lissa thought this quirky. *I do too.*

"Yes. Once out of the elevator I went to the lab door, but the Forensics Department sign was gone and replaced with one which read, "Department of Yesterday." How strange dreams can be, huh? Well, before I entered—for no particular reason—I put on a pair of night-vision goggles that I found in my hands. I walked alone in the dark. I kept the lights off, blinds closed…don't know why.

"Once in the lab, I wandered around searching with neither a destination or object in mind. Then I felt drawn to the specimen drawers in the rear. The edges of one drawer appeared outlined by a thin beam of brilliant light emanating from within. The yellowish-blue light beckoned 'Open me!' I did."

Lars relived his dream, feeling the emotions returning. "On a tray, the folded napkin lay flat and aglow. With tongs I spread it open. My eyes had to adjust to the intense radiance. Like a beautiful sunrise, full of the promise of bright sun-filled day. Surreal is the word….?"

In his exuberance, Lars paused to take a deep breath. "Doctor Ryons, when I stared at the cloth it all made sense to me. In a flash, the words and designs came together and I understood them. I could see through it and comprehend the underside, too!"

Lissa broke in. "Wait a minute. You instantly became super-smart and thought the way the cloth's maker or designer thought? Yikes!" As she listened, her eyes closed to imagine better, her mind cleared and worked at full speed once again piecing his story to her knowledge.

"How amazing huh? Somehow I knew that an astounding intelligence drew these miniature blueprints and plans for something, *somethings* that were wonderful, captivating beyond belief. Oh, and the ink came alive in vivid colors and behaved like blood cells racing through a network of transparent veins. Cars on a flowing freeway.

"For whatever reason and wherever these plans were to be constructed, I absolutely wanted to see the finished results and wished I could be a part of their creation. Then, then, well…I woke up. All the big-picture, intricate comprehension ended instantly.

Zapped away! It seemed like an amazing three hour long dream! Probably only took a few minutes though. I only remembered mere fragments of the fantastic knowledge." Lars gulped after letting this all out. He hadn't gone back to the memory of that dream until right now. At peace, he remained silent, concentrating on the dissipating images. Then he remembered his lone audience.

"Doctor Ryons, before you arrived that morning, out of curiosity, I removed the napkin from the cabinet. I stood over the lifeless cloth on its tray and took a chance. I told everyone to turn off the lights and close the blinds. After that…you know what happened."

Hesitantly, she asked, "Did, did you touch the napkin Lars?" Teeth bit into her lower lip.

"We all did. Oh, now I remember, in my dream the cloth wanted me to touch it. Don't ask me how I knew. But when I did, you might say, gladness filled me like pumping fuel into a race car…well, no…hmm…honestly, I can't describe the feelings."

Lissa was silent. Peace and wonder overtook her while time moved her sideways in a way which drew the scientist to where she'd never gone before. Every second breathed transitioning life to the next conclusion, creating a lifeline of knowledge surpassing everything she'd ever known.

Now, once again, she felt like she did that first night, alone in the lab. *Locking the door, checking it twice, looking back while waiting for the elevator and those foolish thoughts on the forefront of my mind, so much feeling filling my… my what? My heart?*

Now, her legs and voice succumbed to feebleness. Still venturing where she'd never gone before, she believed Lars the only person she could confide in. "Lars, months ago, when I touched the napkin, I, well…you could say that for that brief time, I turned into the best version of myself. My imagination, in a heightened state, zoomed through all past and present relationships while my understanding perceived every aspect in...let's say..." she paused and looked at her shoes. Tearing up, Lissa completed her thought, "the correct way. Oh, I know this doesn't make sense...each needed oil, the soothing oil love brings. Her voice grew faint. Love, yes."

Lars sensed her tender condition and spoke gently. "The best version of ourselves. A good way to put it. Yes, we both experienced the same odd, but wonderful state. Each of us turned from the specimen tray silent, deep in our thoughts."

She recalled her state and softly ventured, "Gentleness."

He thought back and quietly let go, "And Patience."

The feminine voice lightly added, "Gladness."

Lars placed, "Kindness."

Exhaling, Lissa included, "Goodness and appreciation."

The man's voice put out, "Yes. Faithfulness, too."

She inserted, unfolding, "Affection." She pondered, *Self-control?*

With warmth filled confidence he finished, "Peace."

Now Lissa stood still, but amazed within. Gripping her phone, she plunged past her boundary of vulnerability. Half to herself and half to him she asked, "Why was I so affected beyond the level of all of the lab crew? I mean I was the first to experience the...the whatever...the marvel...ousity of the cloth. But, I got hooked, mystified. You know, you saw me. "

Lars' jaw went sideways and he looked up at the ceiling considering this question which required a wise, accurate answer. Confidently, he figuratively stepped near her open heart with firm words. "Perhaps, because you are the most needy of us?"

She pondered this. Half accepting, half uncertain of what his assessment implied. Lissa squinted and then closed her eyes.

Who am I? What am I? I've been acting life out like a wooden figure. A wooden heart? Not good.

The sounds of each other's breathing accented the deepening quality of silence. Though they were in the same building, only floors apart, each was on the other's mind with a clarity in which words were not needed. Both exited the phone call without saying anything else.

Again, Lissa felt herself up against a wall, staring at nothing. Seconds clicked away. *What does matter? Why am I sucked or suckered into this? I have more important, realistic projects waiting for my expertise. I have work to do. Real tangible work! I've flipped out and everyone knows it!* Responsibility faltered and smashed like two protons. Hopelessness, helplessness and powerlessness owned her. In this mental haze she found her 9 to 5 analytical self, wobbling back toward an elusive driver's seat.

Then, someone wandered by in the hall and greeted her. Lissa returned from where her clobbered soul spun. She offered faint recognition to the stranger, then stood up straight and reminded herself that she was a scientist—first.

Professional obligation called. *I've got a meeting to get back to. Let's get this over with!*

Re-entering the meeting room, both men eyed her. Johnson said, "We were getting worried about you, Doctor."

"I just needed to be alone. Also, that was an important phone call from the lab." She spoke with feigned energy in her voice.

Griffin noticed her strange look, but she also, somehow, seemed more attractive and vulnerable. Not so uppity.

Johnson sized up a professional, whose plane of existence had just been her pulled out from under her feet, and replaced by an unexpected, unwanted one. No scorn, all gone.

Lissa thought she must look like a candidate for membership in the A.A.R.P., American Association of Reckless Professionals. *More like wrecked professionals….*

Johnson told her, "By the way, you can thank me for following up on Lucky Luc's advice about that hard-to-find, NASA 3-D Reckoning software. I'm the one who got it to your desk so quickly by having a little more pull than you and the U.N."

Lissa grunted, plus a slight nod in acknowledgement.

I never asked for this...this life. Now, I'm stuck in it. No training prepared me for this. All of my years of education and on-the-job experience, have only left me knowing how one of nature's very wrong turns—a person born as a dwarf—must feel. They host a normal sized brain, in a midget-sized body. She wasn't adapting well to this radical change in reason and authority. Johnson, the bully had won; pounding down a smart and attractive professional woman into a sobbing dwarf, wanting only to leave and live an available normal life.

Her dulled mind existed on life support, surviving as mere mush. She didn't want to sit down, not at that table. Without speaking, she stepped to the small window in the room. The East River sparkled below, surrounding Roosevelt Island and the Queensboro Bridge. *Subways, bridges, tunnels and ferries.* She scanned the metropolitan muddle known as Brooklyn and Queens. She turned back around. The meeting had gone long and the early winter evening took over the city; a clear night with stars. Her flower rested near her laptop and there it stayed. The blossom seemed polluted somehow. Lissa didn't want it near her heart. The beauty of it didn't represent her, and she knew it like never before.

A dream? No. This is real, too real. I'd swap it for a dream in a second! She forced a grin and said in a frank manner, "Gentlemen, obviously we need to talk again. I'm late for some…something. I must say good day." The mouths of both men opened a little. She spun on her heels, laptop in hand. *Hmm, late for something? Y' know maybe I've been late for a lot of things.*

Lissa looked at the pad of paper in her hand. "Inspired" lay in her script. She had no remembrance of writing it. She stopped by her office, dropped off the equipment, got her belongings and left the building without saying anything.

* * *

Joe Fisher's assignment for the day involved janitorial work in the Secretariat's lobby. He noticed an elevator opening. An attractive, but harried, middle-aged woman exited, eyes straight ahead. The overwhelmed look on her face and her sagging posture caused him to shake his head and reflect, *I'm guessin', not a good day for her.*

He reflected on his shift. *Early evening and the place is empty of dignitaries and tourists…good!* He preferred this shift. None of the, *I'm an invisible, anonymous, janitor-at-work state of mind.* Or the repetitious and maddening politeness, "Pardon me, sir. Excuse me, ma'am. C'min' through!" or "Careful there sir, floors still a little wet—see the yellow sign."

During the day shift, Joe impatiently endured common questions by tourists or members of visiting entourages. "Where's the nearest little girls' room? Where's the closest subway entrance? Is the subway safe at night … or ever? Is there a good Thai restaurant in walking distance?" And Joe's favorite—while in uniform and rhythmically sweeping a mop or broom, "Excuse me sir, do you work here?" He had a great answer for that one, but he wanted to keep his job.

Though he had struck up a few relationships with young and sexy U.N. female tour guides, none were on duty now. *Gotta like them short skirts, oh yeah. Them Swedes, whoo-hoo! Those Asians, my, my.*

He didn't speak 147 languages. Most visitors assumed that he must, since he was a U.N. employee. Asians seemed to always ask him the same question. At least, it always sounded the same. Joe had no idea what they wanted and didn't care. He never pursued finding out. Joe put on a fake grin, nodding, until they left him alone.

For all of his efforts, Joe thought he'd probably achieved official "pointer" status. He'd dutifully point foreigners to one of the computer translator stations. Then he'd gesture, air typing on an invisible keyboard, followed by pointing to his eyes with two fingers. After this he nodded, which at such moments, contained an uncaring, pissed-off brain.

On the computer translator screen, visitors could pick the tiny flag icon of a country, then type queries and the answers would appear in their language. *Quite handy,* he thought, *printable maps, too. Now all the U.N. needs to do is make a large sign with 147 languages announcing their locations and purposes.*

He thought, *If I had an almighty buck for every time I was asked a question in some foreign-speak I'd be drivin' a brand new car with a full tank of gas right now! Oh yeah.*

Joe also wished that he could wear his ear buds, listen to some tunes and be in his own world, the United Nation of Joe. But, U.N. policy prevented such a personal luxury for employees in public traffic. But this evening a quiet lobby provided the nice work environment he preferred. Joe concentrated on his job and proceeded through the same course he'd done over the years. He never looked up at the lobby walls or noticed the latest exhibit of 14 framed designs, titled, Napkin Doodle Art.

When his cleaning duties were complete, with equipment in hand, he returned to the mop shop, and went home.

Chapter 26

Dazed, Dr. Ryons made it to her apartment building. Standing on the sidewalk, she fumbled for the entry key. She considered that she had nowhere to go; no friends or family, no dog, no restaurant or coffee hangout; the libraries and museums were too far or closed. She didn't feel like shopping and knew that spending money wouldn't make her better or closer to normal. Lissa gripped her keys, baffled and drained, the scientist trudged up the stairs.

Her pronounced steps alerted Mrs. Roseblum. She cracked open her door. Her head slumped side when she saw Lissa's demeanor. The groan in the old lady was a familiar one, thanks to her long life and myriad relationships. Wearing slippers, she headed for the reclusive female of 2A.

She locked arms with the downcast and said, "Come down to my abode, will you?" This wasn't really a question and Lissa knew that. She complied, devoid of energy to resist. As they entered, the aroma of chicken soup and savory spices stimulated her visitor's nose. Within seconds, Lissa's attitude improved a little though nothing showed this.

Rosie, seeing a far-off look, gently pushed Lissa into a soft, cozy chair. She sat across from her distraught guest. Not knowing what else to say or do, she chose silence.

After five minutes, Dr. Ryons slowly looked sideways, and her eyes drifted, taking in the décor. Using one shoe, she kicked off the other, and then pried that one off with her toes. She sighed and tried to smile, but her face did more of a contortion than a smile.

In her hostess' mind a variety of causes raced from one to the next, ceasing at a mental dead end. Rosie pondered a ritual that could help. She'd fill her large porcelain pot with hot water and add Epson salts and Tea tree oil—it had always calmed her down. Lissa's feet could enjoy the soothing soak. But Rosie thought this too bold for a neighbor she knew so little of. Instead, Rosie filled a bowl with the hot chicken soup. She set a small decorative wood table of just the right height in front of Lissa. No collapsible metal TV tray tables in 2C. Rosie returned with the soup, a chunk of buttered homemade bread and a place setting which included a white cloth napkin.

Lissa took the napkin and held it open to exam both plain sides. *A million plain napkins in this city and I get the only one that, that—*

The hostess eyed her guest's odd movements. Rosie said, "I use pearl onions, cilantro, a dash of red pepper and basil leaves." She tilted her head to catch Lissa's eyes, but couldn't.

The dinner guest sat forward and without expression she methodically ate her meal.

When done, Lissa leaned back. Rosie moved the table aside and hesitantly decided to try a compliment. Grinning, she pleasantly said, "Doll, I've been around and you are the kind of woman that no matter what clothes you put on, you look attractive. Even at my age I'm jealous."

Eyes straight ahead, Lissa gave a stiff, meager nod.

Rosie tried a different tactic to melt the zombie. "Dr. Ryons, eh Lissa, my dear, I know that your job can be a taxing one. How do I know? Well, I went online and scouted out the U.N. websites and some side trails after that. Much of what you do is serious and secretive. Important cases. Must weigh on you some days, no doubt. During the Korean War, I did military paperwork for Uncle Sam—while raising my threesome. I know how only bad news can grind a good heart down. What you do must be a hundredfold of my stint. Besides work, I don't mean to be nosy, I reckon there's no man in your life. No ring, I see. No gentlemen callers. Meaning, probably no romantic pain, eh? If you wanted a fella, a filly like you could get a few easy enough just by shaking your mane. But that is your business. Doll, promise me this, that you won't get caught up defining yourself by your mistakes. That's one long nasty road which is travelled alone. All of that to say, my dear neighbor, you are welcome here." Sincerity spread throughout the room but a bubble of isolation exempted Lissa.

Lissa gave another meager nod and kept her eyes ahead. Quiet minutes passed once more. Then she sagged while her feet fidgeted to get her shoes on. Then she stood with her back to Rosie and hand on door knob. The hostess moved beside her. Lissa spoke, but she did not meet Rosie's eyes. A weak voice trying to sound strong merely said, "Thanks. You have a servant heart. I don't know how that works…to serve others and thrive." She opened the door and noticed a different wreath made of fresh green ivy at 2C. She grinned the barest of grins, *What a nice touch.*

The weary woman, weighed down with unbelievable facts and fiction, made her way down the hall to her apartment.

When Lissa's lock clicked, Mrs. Beverley Roseblum shook her head. After closing her door, she prayed for God's help in Lissa's night. Just then her phone rang, startling her. Within seconds, exuberance and bubbling laughter rose out of her as easily as changing a TV channel. A grandchild had called.

- PART FIVE -

Chapter 27

Lissa fluffed her pillow and closed her eyes again. In the mangle of upsetting dreams, she found herself half-waking and lightly dozing most of the night. *Whoever penned the line, 'Sleep eluded her,' must've been thinking of me! Dawn ain't gonna be no friend of mine.*

After another messy half-dream, Lissa adjusted her position on the bed, plunking her head down on a comfortless pillow.

She dreamed of walking down a narrow dirt path in a field of high weeds. Her sleeve snagged on a thicket. Thorns on the dead branch caught even more as she tried to free herself. When she loosened it, the other sleeve snagged. Each wanted to claim her as their own. After tedious work, both arms enjoyed full movement once more. But, when she tried to go forward, she couldn't. She found one pant leg held by other merciless branches. When she undid these snags, other parts of her clothing caught preventing her advance down the trail. Thorns awaited every attempt.

Lissa sat down to remove a thorny branch stuck on a sock. Then, she crouched and attempted to race through the rest of the trail, hoping to beat the continuing, snatching menace. But, as she leapt forward, she felt the power of captivity surround her and stifle any remaining hope. *I need some snippers or hedge trimmers, no—a chain saw!*

In a twist of exasperation she opened her eyes in her bedroom, a welcomed sight. "No thorns here." Lissa got up to use the toilet, shaking her head. *When is this night going to end? Geez!*

She fell asleep and dreamt again. Hovering above a landscape, she viewed a rural scene. Low hills of vivid green grass soothed her jostled composure. Dark blue clouds, accented by a fringe of puffy white, caught her attention.

Instantly, Lissa liked this place, thinking that anything could happen here. She revived from all of the night's unpleasant scenarios. The sky smacked of goodness, and a yummy flavor rested on her tongue. Enthralled by an airy, omnipresent power running through her, she waited, expecting something good.

Looking down on this new world she wondered, *Now, what's this?* On the horizon to her right, a one-lane asphalt road gleamed from a recent rain shower. The black thread of road pinned to the distance ran close to her vantage point where it broadened from a straight line to a curve and then straight again, off toward another horizon.

Very pretty place, in a simple sort of way. Looks kinda familiar. Is, is…that home? Canada? Indeed, she recalled the location. This stretch of road lay minutes from the farm where she grew up in Quebec.

The sun shone. Rainwater evaporated in a wafting steam from the roadway. A single vehicle drove on the damp asphalt. Lissa was curious about this development. A man in a speeding pick-up truck approached.

Her perspective changed. She was outside the moving vehicle but somehow kept up with its pace. The driver operated the windshield wipers to clear the last rains. This middle-aged man turned his head at something off to his right and broke into a broad smile.

Lissa went wide-eyed. *Dad?* Then she tried to get his attention shouting, 'DAD!' But, this didn't work. So, her eyes followed his gaze to see what absorbed his interest.

Against the dark clouds, just above the wet fields of low meadow grass, a full rainbow of amazing, solid colors, stood proud.

Arc upon arc of the purest hues invigorated her father—and the dreamer. *What a perfect rainbow!* She heard her father express the same words. She chuckled.

Too absorbed in the rare sight, he swerved at the curve in the road and lost control of the truck.

Lissa watched helplessly as her father over-corrected his driving. The truck bounced on ruts in the grass. His forehead banged into the steering wheel, slouched, foot pressing hard on the accelerator. She stayed at the curve, held her breath, as the truck moved at full speed.

In the entire field, only one tree, a large old oak, stood three hundred meters ahead of her father's rig.

He died there.

The scream from her ethereal body escaped her wildly beating heart.

Her eyes opened. The familiar bedroom provided small comfort. Dawn's earliest rays illuminated the apartment. While sitting up in bed, she mused, "He died because he liked a rainbow—rainbows! He couldn't take his eyes off of it, until it was too late! Enthralled by the startling beauty…Dad, I really didn't know you the way I thought I did. You died there…because of a rainbow!"

Eyes tearing up, she processed this new information as if carefully deciding what jewelry to wear to a special evening event. "I was seven years old. It wasn't suicide. No, it wasn't." She heaved a sigh. "All these years…the authorities were wrong…wrong!" She admired her father in oh so many ways. This quick burst of emotion ended with a laugh. She spoke aloud. "He died because of a rainbow…what a way to go!"

As if from the ceiling, Lissa felt a surreal shower of crisp, chill refreshment, gushing over her. This rinsing went deep, removing ugly stains, gritty dirt and the sticky grime of her memories. When the moment passed, she instinctively reached for a handy non-existent towel, feeling an impulsive need to dry off, but she wasn't wet.

Swinging her feet off the bed and into waiting slippers, she still grinned. An inner barrier had blown apart by an unexpected gust of healing lively wind. Now, she could proceed where she'd never gone before. What lay ahead? The thought enticed the sleep deprived traveler.

She held on to this dream so tight life squeezed and intensified. It never entered her mind that this had only been a dream and not a video proving her Dad's innocence. This was real, and no doubts would ever erode the solidity of her wonderfully updated past.

Chapter 28

That day, she wished there was a simpler job waiting, instead of her United Nations post, a job without gripping tendrils of controversy. Lissa decided to be late for work. She emailed the lab about an imaginary dentist appointment.

But first, an unusual urge drew her to go down the hallway to Apt. 2C to tell Rosie about the strange and wonderful dream. She smiled, dressed quickly, anticipating the old woman's sure camaraderie. Lissa briskly made the short walk. With hand raised to give a good knock on her neighbor's door, she froze. A swell of ill rules from a forgettable childhood polluted and dragged down her enthusiasm. When she was seven years old, her father died, due to suicide, and her mother had pounded this shame into her frail youth. Yes, her mother cracked up in her own way. Home held a toxic atmosphere and continual fog of insecurity. Mother was Lissa's enemy. But, mother was her own enemy too.

At Rosie's door an emotional fuse had blown, Lissa shut down. Her hand slunk to her side and she walked away. Not another thought of Mrs. Beverley Roseblum entered her mind. Yet Rosie, with years of sensitivity to the floorboards and elevator ding, knew that someone was walking in the hall toward 2C. She stood up on her toes to look through the door's tiny peephole. Her quick, broad grin changed into an shocked open jaw. Rosie witnessed Lissa's energetic posture, saw it vanish in a moment, and then Lissa vanish too. After the neighbor's strange behavior, she slowly opened the door and watched Lissa disappear down the stairs. Invisible weights caused Lissa's steps to move in an slow motion.

Seeing this, Rosie slumped against her door. Filled with sadness in response, her wondering mind went nowhere, and so she said a short prayer.

Lissa walked to the nearby *Beans 'n Cream, It Seems* pastry shop. Lissa wanted to go to a Starbucks kind of place and just sit there; maybe even try a cup of coffee again—and see what all the fuss was about. Outdoors helped dissipate her heaviness. On the way to the cafe Lissa noticed a bumper sticker. It read "I love my country, but I fear my government!" Chuckling, she thought, *I wish I could buy one that reads, "I love Creation, but I don't trust the Creator!" I'd pay good money for a sticker like that. Maybe I should commission it, sell them and quit my day job?*

After ordering, she plunked down at a tiny corner table. Instantly, she heard the mechanical sneeze of an espresso machine. Overhead, faintly distinguishable music she wasn't familiar with had a style she deemed enjoyable.

A waitress brought Lissa's order: coffee and pastry. She settled in at her table, alone in a crowded, noisy eatery meditating on life for the first time. Yet, she knew by her emotional state, that she wasn't the same Lissa she was just one day before.

Her analytical mind couldn't help but start sizing up the caffeine soakers and pastry lovers. New York City was known to be a microcosm of the world; this morning it seemed so to her. Looking around the room she collected information on these specimens of the human species. Different skin colors, accents and languages she didn't understand. Apparel rooted in far-away countries, cultures and religions. People debating, she couldn't hear about what. Laptops. Laptops. Laptops. Tiny kinds of laptops. And cell phones. Cell phones everywhere. Texters. Texters. Texters. Ear buds in ears. Studious backgammon players. Book and magazine readers. Crossword puzzlers and problem-solvers. A few drinkers read real newspapers and actual paper books. The place buzzed with a unique fusion of humanity anchored at harbor, by food and drink. *Here abides a sampling of citizens of nations, united under one small roof!*

The aroma and noise-filled location exuded life in its busiest and myriad everyday forms. The archipelago of round wooden tables lay defined by their temporary, homesteading inhabitants. *They sail in, they sail out.*

She thought a place like this would make a terrific school field trip. But, the only student on today's trip was one Dr. Lissa Ryons—minus a helpful teacher to explain things.

She wondered who these people were; what kind of jobs they held down. Most of all she considered, *How many of these New Yorkers got on their knees and prayed before leaving their homes? How many said grace or some 'Thank you' prayer before they sipped their latte, and why?*

Over there, that woman. Before she walked out of her house, did she read a page of some cherished sacred text; do some ancient ritual, light a candle or incense before a statue, maybe do a dance? Did anyone rub Buddha's belly? Does anybody still sacrifice animals—hope they don't sacrifice virgins; it'd be hard to find many of those! What makes people tick?

How many begged that a need, want or wish be granted? Isn't prayer just that—begging? Why should we beg for anything from an invisible, laid back, super somebody? Doesn't he, wouldn't he…I mean… his heart already be oh so willing to help us at every turn? She sipped her coffee and chewed her pastry.

There's so much more to do in life than endless religious traditions. Don't they know that? How much is just a religious veneer covering confused or empty lives? Why bow, why kneel? And to whom? Why does "It" want and demand celebrity status…why the religious red carpet treatment?

Tied up tight by what had stumbled into her lab, she tried to sort out what she could. *Is that "thing" going to make me wear certain clothing, follow teachings, or while facing the sunset chant "Hello Universe, yoo hoo, out there!" or something as ridiculous? I better not have to fast—that would make me crazy! Am I going to have to get up early on Saturdays or Sundays? Geez, I hope not, I really like sleeping in. Love bacon, too.*

She turned her observations into self-inspection. *Everyone is so busy at something. What about me? There isn't too much to my life. I'm a loner. I admit it. So! Nobody told me I couldn't be! What's wrong with that? Family? I have some, but I never see them. I think they like their father better...and they can have him. The grandkids? I'm sure they're doing fine without me. Grandma Lissa? Ahh...that just doesn't fit, never has. I keep to myself. I don't bother anyone. They can have their lives. They certainly don't reach out to me, nor I them. Work. Work. Work. I like what I do. I pivot around that purpose—It's mine, I trained for it—It's what I do. Nothing wrong with that!*

Lissa watched the under-one-roof, mini-populace of New York. Her expression evolved into an unpleasant stare. *I don't care about any of these people. And I don't care that I don't care, either!*

Then she choked. Her body rattled, compressed in pain. A swell of unfamiliar emotions sought to burst out of her constricted throat through her tightening mouth. Her sinuses rushed as one, seeking outlets for the liquid via her nose and eyes.

Fearing exposure, her body and soul smote at her calloused, intellectual aloofness. Every inch of her reddened. Vulnerability raced roughshod over her self-centered rationales and excuses. She sat on an invisible sideline bleacher, feeling distant from the capacity crowd of life on the field. *Am I the loser here?* At the same time, fright, a healthy fright, streaked through her. *I don't know how to care! And what would I get out of it, hmm?*

Internally, Lissa clamored for help but didn't remember how to help herself or help anyone else. Her scientific education rose above the unexpected production of tears. She perceived the pooling in her swelling eyelids as containing a unique biological signature, her DNA. Gravity drew a sufficient liquid mass over the round, fleshy edges, passing the fine row of tiny follicles, to a downward path. She knew her body involuntarily produced the liquid…just why, now and here, surprised her.

The teardrops felt hot, striking, captivating as they slowly slid down her face. In that moment, she began to feel like a living component, connected to humanity—at least the microcosm before her. Interest and compassion swelled toward this crowd of nameless people who paused here before further racing in a complex circuit of unknown destinations in the City. The feeling overwhelmed her, she yearned, *I want to join this larger whole.*

A baby cried. *No, more than one—this one is a toddler. Like my youngest grandson Jerry…no, Jared. I should want to see my grandchildren—shouldn't I?* She noticed a babbling young girl running around the edge of a round table in endless circles, while her mother drank from a ceramic mug and ignored her perfectly. The fingertips of the girl's hand traced the circumference and routinely bypassed her busy mom.

This table-looping girl abruptly stopped and stared at Lissa. A few blank seconds passed as they simply looked at each other. Then, without notice, as if someone had cranked the girl's invisible wind-up key on her back, she raced off again, circling her mother's table. Lissa found humor in this. She dabbed her eyes, and chuckled. This genuine laughter in public was the first in weeks, months. In that moment, so much lifted off her, she leaned back in her chair and relaxed. Her legs went limp. Wiggling her toes, she merrily pushed her shoes off. No one saw, no one cared. *I do need to laugh….*

Unconsciously, Lissa's fingertips tapped the table. *Is there a higher-power puppet-master above somewhere, hiding behind a cloud, orchestrating everyone's moves? Are my strings being pulled? If so, why now?* She noticed her jigly fingers' high-paced rhythm. Worried that people observed her, Lissa looked around and gripped the table instead. *No one is watching me.* She let her fingers free.

Is this life and all the emphasis on morality foundationless, hit-n-miss living? Or do absolute truths exist? Who here speaks incantations to ward off evil? Someone once said, 'the biography of the Devil is simply the history of the human race.' Who here meditates on and adores an illustration or photo of a pope, guru or spiritual hero? Does anyone really worship idols anymore? I mean here, in New York? Or anywhere? Is money an idol—our modern idol? Are the media, Internet and entertainment stars the new idols to worship? I mean, does celebrity fandom meet the same needs? Is popularity the same both ways—looking someone up on the Web or the one looked up? If so, gods aplenty.

Lissa sipped her coffee and felt her stomach sending up unpleasant signals. She enjoyed—no, she loved the flavor. But her body treated the dark brew as an unfriendly combatant. She kept drinking. She kept thinking.

What's it all for? All religions can't be right. And all of them can't be wrong—or can they? I don't know if this God is a one-size-fits-all! Or, is the divine bank account actually empty and nobody finds that out until they die? Countless competing religions, humph! Who wants to throw the dice and prayerfully gamble on which teaching is the spiritual jackpot—if any? We smarty-pants humans will scratch an itch until we bleed, oh don't we?

This detour to work has roused my intellect in ways I'd forgotten. The last time I did this kind of soul searching was, was… when? No, it wasn't in high school. No, not a campout under the stars. Well, it was no, not with him either. A date in college? A class? No. It's been… geez, for—never! Never… ever? Her face looked squashed in defeat.

Eating bites of her pastry, Lissa chewed on life. Hundreds of questions waited in line. Yet, tinges of apprehension bolstered any expectation of real answers. *If there is a Supreme Being, he, she, or it doesn't appear to be much of a player. I don't know, how did that Bible story go...after creating the whole world and everything in it, God rested on the seventh day? Maybe he's still resting or just shy? Why allow all this confusion about your identity, unless of course, you aren't looking for attention?* Lissa let out a long breath, which signaled another theological dead end.

Righteous. What does that even mean? Is life a big chess game? Have God and the Devil been going at it through the ages... and I'm just a generic useful or forgettable pawn? I'm certainly not a queen. If that's the game, I hope someone checkmates soon. Working at the Un-United Nations makes me think that could happen any day. Or, is it the Not Ever United Nations? We do so much good at the U.N., constantly trying to counterbalance the continual, non-stop bad.

Nearby, a young woman with a thick, open book, lowered her head, unmistakably choking back emotion. This stranger failed to hold in what touched her and wiped away a tear. Surprised, Lissa found herself wiping away a tear at the same time. From somewhere deep within, empathy welled up seemingly out of nothing. She took a brownish, recycled-paper napkin from her table and placed it to her cheeks and watering eyes. *With a napkin, of all things, I'm absorbing... part of my self. A damn napkin. This is a cosmic joke if there ever was one!*

Suddenly she felt her frazzled emotions rising to an unknown extreme. She daydreamed of standing on her chair in the crowded café and yelling, *You people want to see what a REAL napkin looks like? You should see the one I have in my lab! C'mon and follow me to the United Nations, yeah, that's right! Let's Go! Talk about coffee? I'll tell you somethin' and you won't believe it!*

Then, another daydream caught her attention. Back and forth;

left, right, left, a metronome clicked in a room. In her mind's eye, she watched the device resting on top of an upright piano. On a wood bench, a young girl sat with her back to Lissa. The girl's hands were poised to play. Lissa wondered what her imagination had dreamt up. The girl sat still, waiting, ready. *Whaa—what is she waiting for? Why doesn't she play?* The metronome obediently performed its steady tick-tock, straining Lissa's emotions. *Play a damn song!* The girl half-turned on the bench, and a very young Lissa smiled at the older, adult Lissa. *Huh?* Insecurity swept through her. *What would a shrink say about that?* She took another sip of coffee. *Am I poised to live, in position and ready at the keyboard?*

Without thinking, Lissa reached up to gently stroke the flower normally on her lab coat, but she hadn't been to work yet; there was nothing there.

Her heart and face constricted into a grimace. Any onlooker could've seen her suffering, yet not know the causes. She tried to clear her thinking. *I, I...I've lived on the fringe of the spectrum my whole life, haven't I? There's the other, far side—the destructive, self-centered, yucky people, and then there's me. Isn't there? Those people don't care. They don't care about themselves or anyone else. They end up in jail or live on the streets. I'm opposite them, but still outside of common, human decency, aren't I? Human decency, human decency...I'm decent... aren't I? But, sterile and private, professional and all business. I make an honest living...but, I don't really live. Isn't that okay? No, because I think I've forgotten how or given up on, or... closed the damn door of how to be cared for. Crap! Well, that's nothing to be proud of, my dear doctor.*

Her eyes crossed, she slumped and let out a long sigh. A fingertip pushed an errant drop of coffee on the tabletop, a thin trail followed. Lost at her own island of consumer safety, stark loneliness arrived, and plopped down hard. She considered placing an open hand on the top of her head and pretended that by carefully drawing her fingers into a single large pinch, she could pull out all of the rooted frustrations clobbering her mind. If so, she'd drop this grumbling self-assessments to the floor and achieve freedom. But no.

She sipped, switched gears and changed to the heavy matters waiting for her at work.

I have only one truth, one very crazy, amazing fact—13 billion years. That authenticity began to slowly twist, bend and entwine what consciously made her the investigative person of Dr. Lissa Ryons. For a moment, once again she wished she could be someone else, a person who buttered warm bagels for customers, poured coffee or even washed dishes, something uncomplicated. Something without major implications. *Would you like international unrest with that bagel or a national tragedy for your carrot juice? No problem.*

Surprisingly, she said her first prayer, not even knowing she had. *God, if you made me so bright, one of the sharpest knives in the employment drawer...why did you do—*she could not formulate and finish her grievance.

The hubbub in the café went on. No one knew she prayed a silent request. Unknown to Lissa, the gist of it, born out of her churning soul, had already sped on its way to a distant place where a higher power knows how to fill in blanks and finish incomplete sentences.

I didn't sleep well. Soon, I'll be talking to myself out loud like a strange homeless person. Maybe I should talk to a bizarre homeless person and get their views...couldn't hurt? This city's got plenty to choose from. She stared down at her coffee, shaking her head.

Maybe I should seek out Mr. 13 Billion and see if he'll talk to me. How long does it take a prayer to be answered? Prayer. What is prayer, a religious term for communication? Perhaps he's in the phone book—

toll free, of course? Hah! At this she cracked a smile which lightened her jostled self. A tranquil feeling settled in and she exhaled. But, too soon, a perky waitress stuck her overly interested face into Lissa's private world. The pleasant moment ended like a captured butterfly, whose days of flying were over. With a hard-not-to-return smile, the waitress asked if Lissa would need anything else? No. When the waitress cleared the table she picked up an unused napkin. Written on it was the word "Inspired." Befuddled, the girl cocked her head, watched the woman walk out the door and hosted a short-lived grin.

- PART SIX -

Chapter 29

In hopes to stabilize her mind, while entering the U.N., she mentally recited *My purpose is to provide data and information for evidence based on operational purposes, strategic interventions, policy and decision making.* Saying this mantra helped cleanse away the myriad of frightful thoughts haunting her.

The new security protocols annoyed everyone. Her status as the lone survivor did not come with extra grace and celebrity exception. Even the latest tech scanning machines required lost minutes from everyone. Purses, laptops and an array of unusual possessions from over 100 cultures and 170 countries slowed the security inspections. A world of visitors speaking a world of languages created ongoing challenges for the staff. The U.N. did not employ thousands of versatile interpreters.

When Lissa arrived at the lab, things seemed normal. None of the crew knew about the content of the previous day's meeting, and no one asked. But Lars' expression seemed to hold a sad secret. Lissa eyed him staring at the floor. Before she asked, he went to her and explained that the napkin was "gone; sealed up and returned, by request of one Mr. Donald Griffin. Sent off to the Archives Department...along with the four corners, too. Sorry to tell you, Doctor."

She nodded. *Numb? Yes. Why did I even come in today? I feel useless.* She felt the world turning faster, hitting a speed bump, and no slowing down.

In her mind she navigated to a blurry memory. The end of the first Indiana Jones movie, *Raiders of the Lost Ark*. Empty assurance was given to "Indi" that the government's best people would, of course, be researching his hard-won prize, the golden Ark of the Covenant. This last scene showed the powerful, priceless, ancient, artifact in a generic packing crate, wheeled into a huge warehouse and placed on a shelf among countless other government-owned property. *That's probably the future of my—the, napkin. Top priority, oh yeah! No doubt about that.*

Dr. Ryons went into her office but couldn't concentrate. Her office had never felt so small and the lab nothing more than a high-class burger stand. *All we do is dole out scientific answers to all comers. With or without fries, ambassador?*

She had questions, too many questions, but didn't want answers. She slumped in her chair, realizing that a tray full of Chamomile Shuffles would just sit on her desk until they got cold. *This must be depression. Sucky kind of mood.*

Coworkers glanced at their boss, knowing the missing pet struck hard. The crew couldn't help but notice her chewing on a thumbnail. They shook their heads and dragged feet. They felt loss, like a magical sparkle had spun beyond their reach and left through an open window to the outside world. Gone.

Lissa noticed a bright red carnation waiting for her. *No. Not today.* When she swept it toward the waste basket, it hit the edge and landed on the floor. Dr. Ryons thought twice and decided to leave it there. Shaking her head in frustration, air rushed from her soured lips. "Sorry. Not today."

She recalled how the excited, uplifted feelings had surged in her on that first day, returning to work after the bombing. But this morning, she sat on a see-saw with both feet on the ground and not a playmate in sight. *I'm getting off. Should do something first, though. At least check the email, then I'll go home early… real early!* Her computer came on.

Aside from all the usual suspects stacking up, one message caught her eye. It was from a Professor Luc Sigurdsson. *Damn! No doubt it's really from that jackass Johnson, or that worthless grunge Griffin! Talk about jerks n' tricksters who don't know when to stop.* With a grunt, she deleted the email without even looking at it.

She mumbled, "Internet…inter-schmet." Curiosity raked at her mind. *Fine, I'll do that!* Taking a penny lying on a counter, she positioned it on a thumb and flipped it in the air. *Heads, I look at the pesky email, tails I don't.* Then the telephone rang. Apathetic, she just let it go to voice mail. *I don't want to talk to anybody today.*

Going with impulse, she threw the impartial, innocent penny at the rear office wall. *Worthless, pointless currency, cost more to make 'em than they're worth.* Lissa never looked to see what side the impromptu decision-making coin landed on. The thrust of physical energy felt good though. *Maybe I need to take up racquetball.*

One of her coworkers, seeing the boss under some strange added stress, stuck their head in the office and politely asked if there were anything they could do, even offering to order up her favorite drink. "Chamomile Shuffle—was it?" The doctor couldn't tell you what object in arm's reach she hurled at the sound of where this voice came from, but it flew, fueled by fury. The coworker couldn't tell why he turned into a human target, but he ducked in time.

Flip-flopping, she decided to see what Johnson had conjured up. She opened the Deleted Items folder and clicked on the email. "Professor Luc Sigurdsson, hmm…Okay." On the page she read, "Apologies, Dr. Ryons, for my recent little spoof on you at the United Nations."

Good start! With an uncontainable huff, she continued reading. "Being a messenger, if we wish to, we can use a little of our own creativity in the delivery. I hope no harm has befallen you.

"I know you have found that all I explained in the lobby, and the information we discussed—are facts. It must be a shock to your understanding and education. The four outside sources closely dated the napkin, which I left on the floor months ago by the Lost and Found shelves in the Archive Annex Department. 13 billion years! Quite a lot for you to take in Doctor, but not for me."

She tightened her lips and felt like spitting on her computer screen. "What a bunch of BS!" She read on.

"I know that you acquired the 'Reckoning' software and have turned back the clock of the sky chart to align the key galaxies. They were much farther than you ever would have guessed. I had hinted at the boggling truth with my 'make you cuckoo' comment. My sources told me I would be impressed with your scientific work and natural, keen follow-through."

"What the hell! Piling it higher and deeee…" she trailed off.

"So very long ago—to you—but, like yesterday to us, I was privy to the evolving of those unique ideas, back-to-back, I might add. Then we watched them unfold—literally. Don't be confused; I am not a butler, yet I was holding You-know-who's drink. He drew His plans on what He found handy. You yourself have a favorite liquid refreshment too… Chamomile Shuffle, isn't it?"

This went over the top, for her. Yet, before she closed the letter she noticed a link in blue and decided to click on it and see what other BS lay for her amusement.

"More crap to come, I'm sure! That Johnson character sure missed his calling as a creative writer. I'll definitely let that jackass know." She didn't care if any of the crew overheard her jabbering.

A website popped up devoted to all things, "The Napkin." *Well… this is interesting. Looks like he knocked himself out! My tax dollars at work are taxing my patience.* Making a fist at the screen, she let out a, "Grrr…"

As she navigated, Lissa noticed a link to a variety of videos, all had audio buttons. She whispered to herself while exploring, "First is of my entire visit with Professor Sigurdsson. Seventy-eight minutes, hmm, that sounds about right. There are surveillance selections of the lab tests including the glow. And all of the 14 enlarged sections of the exhibit are here to click on. Not a bad site. So, it looks like the entire chronological timeline and all the so-called facts about 'that clever little napkin' are here, but what for?"

Chagrined, Lissa muttered, "Curiouser and curiouser." After finding a page with a site map, she went to "Transcriptions of conversations…"

Lissa leaned forward in her chair and with a finger traced the variety of choices. A disdain dawned on her face as she started to explore the surprise website. "Okay, wow! There's poor Joe the janitor just doin' his job and stumbling on the beginning of all this business. What else is there?" Shocked, she slapped her desk, "Oh great! We have the video surveillance of the big meeting yesterday. Thank you! I sure want to relive that, over and over again!"

A twisting, wild anger grew. Lissa decided to unload on Johnson himself. Conveniently, his phone number was listed on the site along with Griffin's and her own. "Nice one. Thanks a lot. Just what I need. My photo, name and work phone number on the Web for all to see!" Seething, she grabbed the phone and dialed.

A curt, to the point, man's voice answered, "Johnson."

"So, that is your name or maybe just another ruse, huh!"

"Who is this?" he snapped.

"It's Doctor Lissa Ryons, from the United Nations, remember? From, oh…wasn't it just yesterday?"

"How did you get this number Doctor Ryons?" She heard an odd vulnerability. "It's strictly classified. Now, as you might imagine, I am very busy," he added in a no-nonsense tone.

"The number? No problem, unless you can't read or are blind, I guess! Why do you care, Johnny?" She enjoyed toying with this jerk via phone.

"Maybe your lap dog Griffin gave it to me," She said with a pay-back smile on her face.

"Donald Griffin does not know how to contact me directly, Doctor Ryons, he stated in a matter-of-fact manner, which hooked her attention. "He has to call the Department of Defense operator, leave a message and I phone him back—that's the procedure." His tone of voice wavered between irritation and conditional politeness.

"Okay, Johnny, I'll believe that for the moment." Expressing to him what he already guessed. "Y' know I don't trust you." Curtly, she continued, "Maybe some dumb-dumb put it on the Internet."

He answered, "No, that information has never been online. That's protocol, Doctor. Government agencies such as mine operate in a certain sphere of…" Johnson stopped in mid-sentence wondering why he was even heading down this rabbit trail.

Lissa jumped in, "I actually got it from that website of yours. That gamey, piece of work about a 'soooo clever napkin.' Tell me, Johnny, yesterday did you earn your 'Humiliate a Scientist' merit badge to be a D.O.D. Eagle Scout? Just why did you pick Dr. Ryons, huh?"

"What? Huh? Wait a minute! What are you talking about, Doctor Ryons…honestly?" His voice drenched with sticky curiosity.

From an increasingly aggravated attitude she spat out, "Internet mean anything to you, websites and such? What's your email address, jerk, and I will forward this to you, click on the link yourself. Yeah, as if you didn't know what's coming! Jackass."

He complied, sounding like he didn't know what was going on or what he would see. In a matter of seconds he spoke again. "It's coming up now." Silence followed, then, "Huh? What the –? No! Geez, what the hell!" His voice rose steadily with each exclamation. "Who's behind this? What in the world! When did you get this; I swear it didn't come from me, my office or the D.O.D.! Who sent this to you? What's the name at the Inbox, oh so, it's him, that impostor Professor!"

Exasperation in Johnson's voice made Lissa smile in satisfaction. In a feigned, little-girl voice she slowly unloaded what was on her mind. "Well, to humor you, Mr. Johnson, yep, it came from a 'Professor "Lucky" Luc Sigurdsson', now didn't it? And you've heard of him." Then her voice turned icy. "Nice of you and the D.O.D. to put all this on the Web. What about my privacy and that of my coworkers—jerk? Also, I find it interesting that everything about Project Skedaddle is here for the world to see and be humored by! You even uploaded the surveillance camera footage of our entire meeting yesterday. What's up with that huh?" She was incensed.

"Wait a minute, Doc. Let me look at that, will you? Just h-a-n-g on please!" Silence pounded on her end, and mouse clicking prevailed on his. She heard groans and cursing and a yell, "Charlie, get in here and look at this, right quick!"

Time crunched by. She waited impatiently, hatching plans for vengeance, hardly noticing her toes tapping at high-speed, on the floor.

Johnson came back on the line. "I see the meeting video, 2 hours 13 minutes; you were right. But allow me to straighten you out on a few points, Doctor. There are *no* surveillance video cameras or listening devices in that meeting room. Many of the United Nations meeting rooms have them; it's a long-standing policy. I picked that room for complete privacy. Go take a look for yourself if you want! Also, it would *not* be in my own, or national security interests to advertise my face as a Department of Defense agent, now would it? I'm glancing over the 'facts' about the cloth listed here in the transcript; quite accurate to the letter. What we have here is the beginning of one massive-sized headache."

He paused longer this time and came back with a strained voice, "Ah, oh! The four university laboratories that investigated and dated the specimen are not only named, but their reports are posted in full. More classified data, more and more on every page. Then there's the footage of Joe the janitor's interrogation. There are no cameras in that room either—I was there! Geez, who did this to us and why?" He was sincere, she knew.

Johnson let out a tension-filled, "Good God, there's links to YouTube, Wikipedia, a host of social media networking sites and even a Napkin chat room and who knows what else. Aw, shit!"

There was silence for awhile. Lissa heard him yelling to someone about phoning the C.I.A. *By the timbre of his voice, I'd say he's absolutely sincere. Yes, there are too many professional protocols cast aside for this to have been done by the D.O.D. or the U.N.* Johnson's deep breaths confirmed his refutations.

He came back on the line in a vexed, but inquisitive voice. Perceptively, with a loss for the right way to put it, he questioned her louder than he'd wished, "What the hell were you doing in the women's restroom, having some kind of meltdown?"

Embarrassed, Lissa let that pass without comment.

On her end, she typed "Janitor investigation" in the search box. After watching, she gasped. "You bastards treated that poor janitor that way? Oh, my god!" *Why does it not surprise me that Johnson was in charge with his dog Griffin hoping to sink his teeth in for a juicy bite!*

Johnson spoke. "On the site I've found bio's of me, you, Griffin and even Joe Fisher. Boy, they—whoever they are—didn't miss a step!"

This caught her curiosity. *Too peculiar.* Lissa stopped to read about her own little life. After a while she grunted, "Hmm. Not bad."

She heard a muffled chuckle. Johnson overheard her complimentary remark. He spoke in a barely professional tone. "Think that's a nicety, a perk? Let me tell you something about being in my highly-polished shoes right now—does busily drowning in sheer impossibilities register with you, Doctor, does it?"

Lissa heard hard breathing, deep heavy gasps, more like heaving. He asked, "No joking around now, Doctor, who sent you the email with this link?"

"It's right there. I came to work, turned on my computer and looked at my email. You got what I opened. I forwarded to you as requested."

Failing for words he asked, "Would…did…could, someone in your...lab, nah…maybe…."

"If you're going to accuse someone in my crew…." Her voice trailed off as she added, "I'm getting off the phone now. You know how to reach me."

He weakly said, "And now you know how to reach me." He changed his swirling, over-filled mind, shouting into the phone, "Wait a minute, Dr. Ryons—please!"

She heard voices, muffled sounds and loud commands.

After a full minute Johnson came back on the line. In a tense voice, he stated, "My team is telling me something about the Skedaddle website. It's not traceable to any server, proxy or not, in this nation, Europe, or any source point around the globe. But we will find that server's location. Damn, we will! Luc's anonymity software is good, extremely good. No detectable encryption signature, no code, the site is just there, independent. This one is a new trick for us." He paused a moment, "Ahh…oh! The Home

Page has a Site Visitor Count and its way passed the number 2. In fact, it's revolving as we speak."

"What exactly does that mean?" she asked.

He replied, "It means as of right now, our powers that be, and we are mighty powerful, cannot kill this site, stop it or bring it down. You and I were the first viewers and now this damn cyber-cat is way out of the bag!"

Alarmed, she said, "You mean the U.S. government can't shut it down, pull the plug or anything?"

Johnson said with a huff, "Not right now, no. I am sorry to admit it. Consider this like a new computer virus that'll take time to create a fix for."

Chapter 30

Lissa continued scanning the site's pages and came across 'Blogs.' The list included Johnson, Griffin, Joe, Hammond, Stevens, Lars and last of all hers. No blog for Tiffany, but she had a photo and timeline recognition. *What a charmer she is*, Lissa thought. No blogs or bio's for the dead terrorists. Gee, what a loss, sorry guys. I'm sure you were truly wonderful people in your own special way—like murder, tsk, tsk.

Curiosity overflowed as she silently mouthed the words "Dr. Lissa Ryons' Blog." The first entry began at her apartment before going to work on the very day the napkin arrived at the Forensics Department. Strange, incredibly, the blog was a record, a transcription, of her thought-life related to the cloth. A day-by-day mental diary. As Lissa read, she spurted out "Whaaat!" She half-stood, slammed her hands flat on her desk and shoved paperwork in both directions. The entire world could read her mind. She exhaled a gust of breath, then slumped. In a dictionary, there would've been a photo of her next to the entry "Anguish."

Untethered to reality, tinges, then layers of paranoia settled in.

Her crew heard the commotion. They apprehensively looked toward her office. She scowled, shooing them away with one hand, and sat down hard.

She put her chin in a quaking palm as she scanned the multitude of web pages. *Someone's gone through a huge amount of data and arranged it perfectly. Must have taken days or weeks to build such a site. For what purpose or purposes? What was the napkin really all about? Why are our lives exposed in cyber publicity? Why were none of the players even consulted or asked permission? Why this excess? What is unfolding here? This is one of those things that needs to go wrong—dead wrong and fast! But it probably won't! I don't want to end up on one of those morning TV talk shows or Oprah—is she even on? Are there still any Stone Age tribes in the Amazon that will adopt me?*

Lissa barked at her computer, "They didn't even blur our faces! Everyone in the U.N., anyone in New York City or the world will know me now. What for? Why me? Thanks, Mystery Mischief Makers! I'm not a fan of your trickster know-how!'" She made the bird sign with her fingers and flipped it at the screen. Lissa glared and squinted as never in her life before. She stammered, "I hope the FBI finds you and finds you quick!"

She was about to tell Johnson about the mind-blogs when he spoke in a, "Oh my God!" pitch. "Doc, you really got banged up. I'm seeing you in the hospital." He didn't express it in words, but he mumbled something which she took to be guilt mixed with sympathy due to his impersonal treatment of her during the meeting.

Groaning she exclaimed, "The hospital!" Leaning back in her chair she thought, *I hope there's not footage of me on the toilet or shots of my backside in one of those ridiculous hospital goon gowns. What an under-engineered embarrassment those items are.*

A walking-cane icon appeared in the bottom right corner. "Huh, what's this now?" She clicked. "Mrs. Beverley Roseblum! Rosie was in on this, and Bubba? That's the week I left the hospital." Shocked, after three years as neighbors Lissa had finally gave in, walked in, and drank tea and treats." I'm not so sociable I guess. But, those lemon bars…yum. Lissa watched herself leave. Then months later she saw the downtrodden Lissa, same afternoon of the meeting and her meltdown. "Yesterday. Boy, I was a mess. Look at me. A zombie. My neighbor is worth her weight in bakery goods." I left Rosie's apartment barely saying a word. I return again.

This morning! I stood at the door and never knocked. She knew I was right there—she knew. What an odd twosome. She saw my awful expression. My dear harmful mother really messed me up. And, and, what's this, me all muddled leaving the building. She's praying for me again. Oh my God. I guess that's a good thing? I need to forgive—my terrible mother. That woman emotionally robbed from me."

Johnson said with a half-hearted sounding can-do attitude, "Listen up, Doc. The IT guys will crack this fancy spoofery, this latest cyber attack on the United States government and the U.N. We'll get the terrorists responsible for this embarrassment. These goons are one complex and intrusive bunch of nuts. Plus, if our much, much informed impostor, Luc, isn't an ongoing, escalating threat to our national security, Project Skedaddle goes to a different department than my own. The D.O.D. will assess what other penetrations and threats this group has accomplished and find out what their demands are."

Lissa interjected, "But Mr. Johnson how could these cyber-terrorists record where there aren't cameras or microphones? Doesn't that alarm you? Did they use for-hire, precision psychics?" She stiffened, feeling frightfully like that helpless, conscripted pawn in a game of celestial chess. "I don't like saying this, but what if—well…maybe some kind of crafty mystical, supernatural or extraterrestrial powers are at work here? Doesn't all this mysterious invisible hardware prove some higher power or space aliens are behind this?" But, she assumed if the government knew of the presence of little green men from Mars, Johnson's paycheck equaled him playing dumb.

He answered. "Doctor, the general public has no idea what toys we in the military have to play with. Sorry if I sound condescending, but if I told you one-tenth of the technology we use for prying eyes and listening ears, it would make your hair stand on end and your toes curl, and I'd lose my job." He added, "Mystical? Invisibility cloaks? Chatty angels? Religious mumbo-jumbo. You can go there if you can't help yourself; just leave me at the train station. Knock yourself out, go opti-mystic. Enjoy your entertainment of myths, legends, fairy tales, kiddie fables, Harry Potter, oh … and those late-night radio talk shows."

That response troubled her. *Grr… opti-mysticism, yeah, yeah, so smart.* It sounded like good ol' one-sided boasting. The phrase, narrow-minded, took up residence in her evaluation of him. *The Great and Invincible United States of America will not be undone, we are unstoppable!* Such reinforcement from him would require more than this one long, wobbly stride of believing for her. The U.S.A., not being her native country, she reminded herself, was known for cover-ups of screw-ups, and screwing up the cover-ups.

Lissa recognized doubts growing in her mind. A line-up of what seemed like logical protests, *But, wait! But if…! But… how?* And a second line-up of *Then ifs!* not far behind. She had her reservations. *But, what do I know of espionage and spyware? Geez, we are both professionals, not dummies—that's for sure. James Bond 007 and Jason Bourne, where are you?*

Open-minded, but perplexed, she didn't understand why this was happening. Looking for a simple explanation Lissa said to Johnson, "What's going on here? Why are we being treated this way? What's anybody got to gain from all of this? If there's something you're not telling me, maybe now is the time to let me in on it?"

Helping her understand the mystery, Johnson confided, "Obviously, someone in the U.N. with security clearance is working with this bunch, which bothers me to no end. That person or persons, has good connections. And I don't mean only electronic access. This is a serious breach in the core of the world's meeting place. Not good, not fun. That's why U.N. Security contacted us, the D.O.D. Suspicion swirls around that international complex on a day to day basis. We're the host country and can't have a wild card or loose AK-47 spitting there. Beyond that, Doctor, I cannot tell you how, when, where, and what functions U.N. Security performs. You are the last person I need to remind of the recent bombings of where you are employed."

"Gotcha!" She had put so much emphasis on Muslim extremists, she forgot how many other politically motivated murderous types or mental screwballs inhabited the world. Once again, she considered the Christmas Bombing. *I could've died that night—one more ornament on their terror Christmas tree. But I survived, why? Why wasn't I number 48 in the fatalities? Does this website…well, yes…I have been invisibly stalked for months! Geez! I've been someone's prey for their own ends. Ohh, oh.*

Her racing thoughts now intersected in one unpleasant central place. Lissa stood on the edge of a long, narrow pier of sorrow. She leaned hard on its wooden railing. Her eyes stared out and saw much too much pain even from her limited vantage point. Queasiness vied with aloofness for position in this personal upheaval. *I'm not safe anymore, am I? Great!* Lissa took this in. *I wasn't safe before, but I didn't know it until the bombing.* She now considered the website and all that came with it, from this new, suffocating view.

More goes on with the *shadows* than she ever conceived. Maybe in the past, while tapping on her laboratory walls, she simply hadn't hit the right place after all.

Hesitating, she eyed the ceiling and said, "Johnson, are…are there any spiral stair—? Oh, never mind."

She took a deep breath and wondered. "So, that's why I got my funding, huh Johnson? My ideas and efforts to advertise the mysterious napkin were approved, backed, and funded because of…you? The graphics, the websites and prizes, three lobby exhibits…oh my God! You! Those were implemented to drop bait to attract a terror cell or a crazy…you were fishing for a lead or a goof-up on their end…well, I'll be damned!" Technological pin-pricks caused her pronounced deflation. Her dedication to the really weird mystery was handed to her on a silver platter covered over with cheap tin foil. *Time to wad up that shiny veneer and toss it in the garbage.*

"Bingo! But this time we're really in the bingo hall, Doctor. All the Internet traffic funneled our way for deeper analysis. The webmaster…well, you could say, is on the payroll." Johnson paused to sip some coffee. She heard a couple slurps and couldn't help but wonder if that was a coffee cup he had in his hand.

"Yes, we wanted to draw out any crazies—like the bombers, hackers or stalkers—whoever. We couldn't expose our secrecy to you." He paused and sipped once more. "We hoped to track and implicate suspicious persons, if you will, before they could carry out any criminal activities. That's my job."

She wondered what part Don Griffin played in all this. "And Mr. Griffin?"

"Mr. Griffin knows only what he needs to know. You will be pleased—since you described him as a 'lap dog' that he's on a nice short leash." A grunt followed his brief explanation.

The annoying meeting was fresh on her mind. "Why did we have the meeting yesterday? I mean you obviously read all my files and secretly visited the lab specimen after hours. What was left?"

Johnson was quick to answer. "Two issues, Doc. First, we wondered if you might've had any undocumented theories to air concerning any aspect of the Skedaddle Project. But, second and more importantly, you withheld potential evidence in a terrorist bombing by not reporting the luminescent property of the cloth. Our lab boys are still not sure why.

Lissa sunk low in her seat. *Oh boy. So, that finally came back to bite me.*

"Oh, then there was your questionable adoration of Saint Luc." He grunted out, "Suspicious activity for the Chief of Forensics, wouldn't you agree? We also found it interesting, or perhaps, convenient is a better word, that you made it out of the U.N. building seconds before the attack—as if on cue. Dr. Ryons, you were a suspect—briefly. In cahoots? Honestly, we'd didn't want to think so. We dug deeper into your past and shopped your photo to local mosque infiltrators…but, I didn't just tell you that did I?"

She sunk even lower. *Mosques. I don't even believe in a God or any of those ancient books.*

"That's behind us now, and you've been cleared of any criminal association. They infiltrated the U.N. Doctor, this astrophysicist imposter either works with a mole—meaning a spy—at NASA, or is one of Luc's comrades, or perhaps he himself has fooled his way in to a NASA facility and now operates in their system. Possibly they hacked 'em good. From our experience, an old guy like Luc is never alone in these espionage operations. That unknown person made the drop at the Lost and Found."

Lissa winced. Curiosity moved her, "Drop?"

He answered, "The dictionary definition? Let's see." Keys clicked. He quoted, 'A predetermined suitable place for hiding something such as the deposit of illicit goods or intelligence information.'"

Lissa stared at nothing and found it hard to breathe. She heard a faint repetitious sound and looked for the source; she was irritated to find both her fingernails and foot doing some high-speed drumming. She stopped, only to begin again when she spoke. Deflated, she crept out of her deep thoughts. "So, that's how Prof…I mean Luc, or whoever he is, that's how he knew of the special 3-D Reckoning software—illegally?"

Johnson flatly answered the unpleasant truth, "The only way."
He followed up. "Don't be too hard on yourself, Doctor Ryons.
He appeared to have an answer to your deepest curiosity. The
Professor made a good mix of science fiction with science fact. Oh,
he was good—one helluva actor, gotta love that accent. But, yes,
they recruited you for this hoax. We have forwarded NASA several
photos and voice prints of our darling Professor. Unfortunately, we
couldn't get a decent set of fingerprints. The reception counter and
commissary table surfaces were fingerprint puzzles. His business
card included yours in that tiny puzzle. We could get not a one."

Lissa didn't know her body could slump so low into the position
she found it in. "Then Project Skedaddle is closed? I mean, did you
get what you wanted?"

"We didn't get enough, but we got some. And, as we say in this
business, 'that's plenty more than we used to have!'" He carefully
worded his next statement. "Please consider the limits of what
I can and can't say to you, plus what I personally feel the U.S.
government owes you, Doctor. This will all be in my…and I do
mean this sincerely, confidential report. But, understand Doctor
Ryons, whatever intel the D.O.D. gained will now move on to
another department and other agents. Honestly, I may never know
what the data mining reveals about this caper."

She wondered, "And what about the C.I.A.s involvement?"

"That's classified."

Lissa thought that sounded like the generic spiel for the prying
taxpayer. *Government mumbo-jumbo, woe-woe. Our tax dollars hard
at work, yea, Go Team!* "So, this Skedaddle Project might end as
nothing but a wild-goose cheese? Ah, I ah, mean chase, a wild
goose chase?" Lissa bit her lower lip and rolled her eyes around.

He answered, "If you're wondering, the former exhibit of the
Children's Plight in Ethiopia or wherever it was, is being held

in close storage ready to bless those walls again." In a whimsical chipper tone, he added, "Oh! If you'd like to adorn the walls of your summer villa or apartment in New York with pieces from the Napkin Doodle Art exhibit, they'll be going pretty cheap, real soon!" Now he'd really blown it with her, and didn't even know it.

Empty seconds passed. She heard a phone call come into his office which he said required his attention. He put her on hold. During these seconds Lissa began to feel more like herself. All the god-ish and mystical possibilities left her. The mystery? Just uncommon criminals. She looked forward to the concept of getting back to work again.

Johnson returned. "Still there? Between you and me Doctor, if this napkin business had, and I do emphasize had, proven to be an out-of-this-world phenomena, you'd never hear it from my departmental salaried lips, nor would you be reading about in the newspaper."

She couldn't help but think, *Area 51 all over again. Thank you, Uncle Sam!* Then she had a mental hiccup. *Depart and mental. Yeah, I wonder how much Johnson has departed from-his-mental, working for years in his suit and well-heeled patriotism?*

Lissa remembered the "planted" napkin and the glow, plus the pleasing effects. At this, a small box appeared on her computer screen. She started watching a video of herself in the darkened lab discovering the napkin's unusual properties. Fingertips touching the glowing cloth, then her pulling away, contemplating the object. She heard her own recorded sigh. *Did I swoon? Is that what I did? My, my. I forgot what an impact the touch…well, look at me overwhelmed. Geez!*

The unseen, attentive filmer had zoomed in on her. A countenance of soft pleasure, an enviable contentment rested on the face of the scientist. *I'd sure like to feel that way more often, everyday wouldn't be too much.*

She watched herself slide the specimen tray into a drawer and walk away. Hidden from view, except from an inside shot, the napkin changed. Specks of bright gold appeared lighting up the area within the drawer. Outside the specimen cabinet, a fine brilliant line of light illuminated the gap around the rectangle. Watching the screen, Lissa mouthed, "What the…?" A gold spark raced through each dark blue letter to the end of every section of written information. Without noise, like two dozen lit fuses, each character of the odd language lived, glowed in pride and then subdued to its previous dull state. Like glittering messages or words made out of sparkling fireworks; come and gone. *Huh? How did that get filmed?*

Lissa stared at the screen, shook her head and leaned in further, uttering, "Well, I'll be. So, five seconds after I turn my back—it does this! Humpf!" Her mouth stayed opened in shock, while her finger pointed to the phenomena she missed. She considered pressing the handy replay button, but waited for another, perhaps different light show.

That little bast—. She leaned back, folded her arms and squeezed her body tight. Insecurity took a deeper spin, further spiraling her sanity down to a place she did not want to go. Nothing could stop the momentum. A dormant part of her psyche erupted, confirming this uncomfortable paranormal truth. Both of her hands shook. Lissa stared at the obvious symptom of internal instability.

How did this light show fit into the equation, why all the colors anyway? Originally, the glow tipped her off that the cloth held something inherently unique, perhaps...with unknown... potential...of what? She didn't know. Now, with Johnson on the phone she hesitated to pin him down and hear his explanation. In this round of playing cards, she was nearly out of moves. Since he didn't bring it up, she assumed he already had a rebuttal in the ready. She guessed he'd say, *A simple side effect of a unidentified chemical compound whose age can't be dated. He would probably label it as mere window dressing or a nice added touch.* So, she dropped the question.

Lissa did have one other question; her final card. "Okay, thank you so much, Mr. Johnson. You've opened my eyes to what I wouldn't know otherwise. Also, I sincerely appreciate your candor. But, one feature is still puzzling me. How could these webmasters know and accurately record all of our thought-lives, and in real-time?"

Johnson went silent.

Another pressing phone came in; he put Lissa on hold.

Chapter 31

She scrunched up one side of her face. *How did these strangers do that? Not even science can accomplish such a thing in a controlled laboratory setting. I mean, the knowledge of how the human brain functions is more foreign to us than what's on the bottom of the world's oceans for god's sakes!*

As each new technological bafflement settled in, her basic skills of reasoning splintered further and farther apart. A pencil in hand tapped out a fast-paced beat on her desktop. She didn't hear it.

During her time on hold she found one of the Skedaddle web pages with a different small video running in the right bottom corner, about four inches square. A second box next to it showed an empty desk. She peered closer at the first one. The image was her. *Geez, I'm popular!* Then she backed away and noticed her image had changed posture at the same time. She closed in again and her face on the screen enlarged. She stiffened and instinctively tilted backwards. *What the … .*

Lissa stood and looked out her office window. No one in the lab was watching. She used her hand and waved at the screen. The miniature Lissa waved, too.

She looked at her webcam eye and saw that the light was out. She took some masking tape and covered it anyway. Nothing changed. She turned around while eyeing the screen. *Yep! I'm streamin' live to the world. Great! Just great! Gotta love these guys, so caring about details.*

Johnson returned to the line.

In the middle of his first words, Lissa calmly interrupted him. She feared "they" would overhear her. In a hushed voice she whispered, "Johnson, stop. Go to the page titled, 'Today.'"

"Why, what now? Where's that one?" He came to it after a moment. "So, what?"

She answered, "Look to the bottom right corner."

Mildly concerned, he asked. "At the two little videos…what are they of?"

"It's you and me talking—live!" she said lyrically with a smirk.

"Just turn off your webcam, Doctor. I'll turn my…I, yi, yi. I don't have one on this computer!" Brooding he leaned back in his chair. She thought, *I see you l-e-a-n-i-n-g…*.

"Mr. Johnson, mine is off and I covered it up, too. Surprise! We're on candid cameras!" She smiled at him and waved, "Oh, hello! My goodness, you don't look so good over there. Kind of took the wind out of you?"

"Candid what?"

She smiled. "Oh, must've been before your time."

Obviously out of patience, she saw and heard him spit out, "Shhh! Just shut up for a second, Doc!" He looked at the small images and teetered his head one way and then the other. The little Johnson followed along. "We're on damn f'in camera! Aww…hell, no!" He paused, "I am not liking this."

He peered below his little box and saw something moving… it was letters. He noticed the invisible typist stop and Johnson mouthed the words there, *I am not liking this!*

"I am definitely not liking this!" followed out loud. The new declaration typed out immediately.

Another not surprising, pressing phone call put his fit on pause. Before he placed Lissa on hold she heard a very different tone in his voice and heard, "Yes sir! I know. I'm seeing it myself. I am actually seeing myself talking to you, which is now streaming on this darn site! It's like a damn reality TV show, but on the World Wide Web."

Lissa noticed a third small box had appeared. A very angry man, of bold demeanor, sat at a desk and looked at himself looking at himself. He then put out his hand over his image on his own computer. Lissa muttered in a quiet sing-song voice, "Won't w-o-r-k!" *Watch the audio guys, the world is listening and reading!* Lissa sized up this new player. *Probably Johnson's boss.*

After a few minutes Johnson returned to the line out of breath. He sputtered out a, "Hang on, Doc." Then he queried her. "I suppose you heard all that?" His breathing and words sounded sluggish and labored. The third video box only showed an empty desk and chair.

"Yep! Loud and clear through my little Bose speakers. But, I didn't follow along because it felt like eavesdropping." Symbolically, a brilliant light bulb lit up over her head. Lissa even reached up to see if she could feel it. She spoke with conviction, "Johnson, all this time someone's been eavesdropping on us! Crap. I'm no lip reader but I could've guessed what your boss was saying even with the sound off...but it was typed too."

Secretly, Johnson admired the ingenuity of this pirate website. He had never seen any site that was so easy to navigate, had great photos, high-definition video, easy to read transcripts, perfect timeline and fonts, instant messaging, proper bios and an untraceable IP address. A moment later these thoughts appeared transcribed on his screen.

Lissa interrupted his thoughts and interjected, "You are jealous! Quite an enemy...no traceable IP address too, hmm!" She looked at his face, and after reading he shifted his eyes to look at hers. He then looked back at his box and read the transcript of his thoughts below it. Instinctively, he threw his hands up feeling robbed.

The doctor ventured, "Yes, I have that same feeling—robbed! But, our robbers are still robbing us. My identity, my privacy, my inner privacy and probably my bra size! All there…all there. Oh boy!"

Someone who looked like an aide of Johnson's entered into the viewing area. This man briefly glanced at the screen and then bent down to whisper in Johnson's ear. After a few seconds of this, in mid-speech, Johnson abruptly moved his head aside. In an annoyed voice, he nearly shouted, "You don't have to whisper dammit! They can hear everything, they know everything we're saying and what the hell—even thinking. Look!" He shot his arm out and pointed to the small box on the screen. The aide moved closer to see better. He saw his own face and below that, the end of the real-time transcript, "Look!"

In another box he also saw a woman seated at a desk looking at him. Relaxed, she eagerly waved and whimsically smiled.

"Oh boy!" He stepped back and folded his arms. After staring for a while, he instinctively let loose one hand and waved. Then he made a wide diameter, clockwise motion. Seeing himself, he then did the same hand motion counter-clockwise and grinned as if he accomplished a unique feat.

Johnson shouted, "Will you stop that!"

"Sorry, boss. It's just so strange. Well, as I began to say, there will be a meeting at eleven-hundred hours in the briefing room of all department heads." Chuckling he added with a grin, "And I guess our friends here, will be coming along!" The assistant was about to exit, but again peered at the three little screens. Above each one were the full names of who was present.

"Oh no, I don't want people to start calling me 'Percy.' My

middle name, and one very well-kept secret!" He stomped out of view. Lissa smirked; a little laugh soothed her.

Johnson needed to get Doctor Ryons off the screen and off the phone. So, he made his closing speech.

Amused, Lissa said, "Oh, I got it already. Time for me to go, huh? Not a problem."

"Ahh…huh? Oh yes, forgot. Yes, time to tackle this dilemma at hand. To sum up the fine points before I go, Doctor Ryons. I am an agnostic. A napkin that science tells me is as old as the universe itself does not tell me there is a God or Creator. But it does tell me to get back to work. Meaning other business and ah…hem, pressing work, the kind I normally do. National security, things which a bullet can stop...that kind of situation. Comprehend-a-a-y? Right now, this doesn't add up to 'anything,' but a mystery." He lowered his face and came back with a deep searching expression. Honesty on his face he asked, "Laying my cards on the table, I don't know what this is, do you Doctor? I got guesses. That's all I got."

Lissa hesitated to ask, "Mr. Johnson, what did the Skedaddle Napkin have to do with the bombing of the U.N.? What's the connection? I mean the first time, well, the word I'd use is interaction—when the first interaction happened with the Napkin, the attack occurred. Y'know, within the hour."

Johnson stated, "I'm unsure if a link existed. My people made no connection. Nah, you think radical Islam…no, no I don't. They made their point, as they've done too many times over the world. Just another big target this time. But, if you see something, Doc, I'm all ears."

Dr. Ryons winced, shook her head and wore an empty grin. "No. I don't. But you've explained plenty and I appreciate that." *Me, a suspect! Whoops! He'll see that. Darn.*

He took a breath and continued. "Not a problem. But, tell me Doctor, does God prefer decaf or regular? Sweeteners? Sugar? Half and half, or black? Sumatran or French Roast?" Then he sipped.

She hesitated, gathering a worthwhile—*was it a rebuttal?* "I see that you yourself, like one of those choices don't you, Mr. Johnson?"

He answered, "Yes, black. Other than that, I don't give a shit as long as it's hot and tastes like coffee! Excuse my French."

She would've bet her paycheck that he was a plain, black coffee, Styrofoam cup guy.

"But Doctor, does this cyber trickery and unanswered questions prove that you and I were made in the image of the so-called Almighty, simply because we occasionally drink a cup of Joe? Pure conjecture isn't it, like all religiosity and spirituality? Don't some religions ban coffee drinking—must piss God off, huh?" He paused, squinted and looked her hard in the eye.

Lissa heard a firm, "Gotta go, Doc." Click.

After that, Lissa decided to finish reading the rest of the email from Luc the Spook. She knew now that her original shock and anger toward Mr. Johnson belonged elsewhere. At her Inbox she scrolled down past dozens of emails from strangers who had just made quite recent visits to the Official Napkin website which prompted their curiosity to contact a Dr. Lissa Ryons. She ho-hummed, "Oh yeah, I forgot my email is out there now, too. Lots of fun ahead for me, thanks to that very clever napkin. "

"Let's see the rest of what the Spook wrote to dear ol' me, his favorite scientist in NYC. She read to herself, "I know fairies aren't real. My comments at the United Nations must have, no doubt, caused you some mischief. When we visit Earth, 'wings' are optional. So, when I visited you, let's just say, I left my wings temporarily behind. But, they are literally behind me again as usual." Here she saw a yellow-faced Emoticon, smiling and winking.

"That's how we get around up here. If you want, you can see me with them on. At The Napkin website locate the "Where It All Began" menu and scroll down the page to "Placing the Napkin." Lissa clicked on the link and followed Luc's instructions. *'Luc'* she thought, *What kind of name…?*

There, at the Placing the Napkin video she watched a glowing being, which resembled a young, stout, and much taller version of Professor Luc Sigurdsson, "Not of Luxembourg," she murmured, "huge wings and a-to-die-for-sword included, WOW! That thing was here at the U.N.?" She gulped. "That creature fears not one thing in this world or his…what a confident look on his face." She zoomed in to look at his face and the jewel-encrusted hilt. What detergent do you use to get a robe looking that white!

From the back of her mind, a thought came closer. She mentally reached for the unknown and curious clue. In a rush Lissa yanked open the top drawer of her desk. "Got it!" The small white feather spun between her pinched thumb and fingers. She stared wondering where the feather came from? *Another world? Another dimension? Where? And when was this placed here for me to find?*

On the computer screen a large yellow smiling emoticon appeared. The grin expanded; went small and repeated. She smelled the feather. "Smells like somewhere nice."

She realized that he, and it, were supernatural. *Must be. Must be! Must be!* Letting go of the feather, she slapped the table top with both hands. Shouting, "I talked with him, too!" Everyone in the lab turned, looking her way, with puzzled expressions. "I talked with him…an angel…or whatever! Wow!

"Wait a minute, I've got a hunch about something." Clicking on the walking-cane icon she navigated back to her first time in

Rosie's home. Lissa watched for the moment when sitting and she had a shock go through her. "Like a strong shot of static electricity. I remember looking around to see if someone did something to me." She noticed how her heart dwelt on her decision to forgive her ex-husband, the father of her estranged children. "Whoa!" At that same moment, at Rosie's, Luc the Angel appeared. In one hand he held a gnarled-handled, glowing, tall wooden staff. Lissa exclaimed, "Geez, does everything they have glow?" Then the angel tapped her spine with his staff. "I think he kind of strengthened or validated my decision by that jolt."

Smiling with glee, legs outstretched, Lissa twirled around in her office chair. Then, grinning, facing her computer, she rocked her head side to side pondering that very clever napkin. *He laid that strange, no...peculiar...no, astounding, yes, astounding ornament from another world on the dirty ol' floor of the United Nations building... why? But, why make such an unannounced, unnoticed divine flourish? So, is...that piece of cloth sacred? I've never considered anything sacred in my life. But, this sure is!*

She couldn't help but be overcome with feelings of specialness. For the first time the woman sincerely considered a throne-world with a God-person and a universe of mysteries. *Mysteries to mere humans—he's the one who makes 'em.*

So, this, his mission, was from his boss...his creator. Certainly not my creator—my father and mother made me—they didn't need anyone's help for that. Did his boss, the coffee drinker person, sculpt this whole plot and choose the cast? Darn! When did I audition for my role? In a warped way, I feel chosen. Me. What's ahead then?

A banner with bright glowing colors beckoned her to click on it. This opened a new video box. She saw herself ignorantly walk out of the U.N. the night of The Tragedy. Knowing what came next, she hardened hands into fists. She shook one at the screen, her throat and face stiff. When she saw herself reach the taxi a bright glow surrounded her. "Whaa?" She leaned in to see better and then saw a magnifier icon appear. Without considering the implications she simply said, "Thank you."

The tall being made of light crouched and covered her with its powerful wings. The brilliant flash of the explosion happened. Then static.

Dr. Ryons' jaw dropped. She jumped out of her chair. One arm shot out with a finger pointing to the static. This realization burst through every cell which made her who she was. "He—he—that thing, that angel—he, he saved, protected me. I'd be dead. Right now dead. He pressed my head down too." Dr. Ryons spun around amazed. In an odd way she accepted the truth that she was special. *Me! An angel was assigned, assigned to me, to save my life... but why?* Then she looked at who was in the lab. No one there noticed the wonderment which had lit Lissa up like never before in her entire life.

On her screen a life-sized white feather floated from the top and out of sight below. Like a screen saver, one floated followed by another. She stared mesmerized.

While considering the computer screen's little surveillance show, she had half an idea. She started to bring up her Project Skedaddle folder and search for the reports from the linguistics code-breaker team. Her eyes scanned, looking for something—it was a word, one specific, curious word. Finally, her racing thoughts cleared. She realized what was bugging her and so typed "Skedaddle" in the Search box,

Her computer brought this up: "In referencing ancient texts, the Book of Genesis was helpful."

Oh, great! Bible-talk, just what I don't want!

She read on. "The description of God's creation of the heavens and the Earth, 'In the beginning ... God spoke light into existence.' This dispelled or caused the darkness to skedaddle ...." She recalled the briefing, and how Griffin nervously called it sheer coincidence how the computer randomly named the project.

Hooked, Lissa went back to the email from the angel-man and read the final line: "Tag! Lissa Ryons, you're it." A new expressionless, yellow-faced Emoticon stared at her. She reached to where a flower normally ornamented her. Without petals to grip, she reached for the cast off creation on the floor and pinned it on. She did not want to fail this opportunity. "I want to be like a flower!"

Instantly, the Emoticon face smiled and winked.

The End

Afterwords & After Thoughts

On the shores of a wide river, a man found a long stick. With arms extended, he held it firm. When he made the tip lightly dig into the moist earth he closed his eyes and pivoted, creating a wide circle. Next, he drew five, angled, straight lines. He didn't know it, but the symbol had been repeated across the face of the earth throughout time. This person stood in the center of the newest pentagram.

Dropping the stick, his eyes and arms then reached upward. A small group surrounding him chanted. They called out, requesting neither a reasonable nor unreasonable devil—something in between. Each wanted a god, a force or spirit bigger than themselves, so they could worship and bow in the shadow of strange greatness and receive protection.

Days, seasons, and eventually years eroded the unholy lines which creased the shoreline; the mark forgotten.

Over 300 years later, surveyors, developers and architects arrived carrying a hefty purse filled with contributions from many tribes, peoples and nations. One of the men pounded a wood stake into the ground, puncturing exactly where the ancient design once had lain and many feet once stood. All smiled. Handshakes sealed the deal and a shovel sliced the earth.

It was 1948. The United Nations complex of buildings grew; girders reached upward. Those surrounding the project came from many lands. In their languages, all chanted heartfelt sentiments, good wishes and hopeful desires.

God looked down and noticed this latest scheme of humankind. He remembered the curse soiling this ground and the incantations spoken by those turned to dust. While watching, He rested his chin on his galaxy-wide palm. After contemplating what to do, He came up with a solution and decided to allow man this new marvel. But one day, inside its corridors, He would send someone to walk and leave something which didn't matter to Him anymore. Like most items that belong to Him, which He leaves behind, He does so with purpose.